The Scorekeeper

a play

SCOTT D. RUSSELL

Visit our website at www.stillwaterpress.com for more information.

First Stillwater River Publications Edition 2020.

Library of Congress Control Number: 2019917521

ISBN-13: 978-1-950339-52-5

1 2 3 4 5 6 7 8 9 10

Written by Scott D. Russell.
Published by Stillwater River Publications, Pawtucket, RI, USA.

Publisher's Cataloging-In-Publication Data
(Prepared by The Donohue Group, Inc.)

Names: Russell, Scott D., 1945- author.
Title: The scorekeeper : a play / Scott D. Russell.
Description: First Stillwater River Publications edition. | Pawtucket, RI, USA : Stillwater River Publications, 2020.
Identifiers: ISBN 9781950339525
Subjects: LCSH: Ruth, Babe, 1895-1948--Drama. | Space and time--Drama. | Pens--Drama.
Classification: LCC PS3618.U7667 S36 2020 | DDC 812/.6--dc23

For Peg
My anchor and my strength.

For William Francis Lee, Jr. & Paula Lee
For raising a wonderful son with a moral consciousness.

For Dr. Vladimir Privman and Dr. Violetta Thierbach
My favorite people in the universe.

"Those who don't believe in magic will never find it."
~Ronald Dahl

"In the magical universe there are no coincidences and there are no accidents. Nothing happens unless someone wills it to happen."
~William S. Burroughs

"Children see magic because they look for it."
~Christopher Moore

Preface

In 1973, my fifth major league season, I met Scott Russell, a mild-mannered superstar of baseball statistics way before Bill James. Scott's research clearly proved the immediate and practical impact of blacks on the game of baseball. Scott's comprehensive study conclusively proved a sustained statistical superiority once these blacks and Hispanics were given the opportunity to compete with their white counterparts.

Little did we know at the time, that Scott's other statistical studies would eventually spawn today's often senseless and mind-numbing analytics, a situation that has "evolved" into a current foolishness that has permeated major league broadcast booths, and even more sadly, baseball front offices. All this because Russell attempted to decisively prove why my ERA was higher on artificial turf! Today we are bombarded with how left-handed pitchers fare on Wednesday afternoons versus hitters of Armenian descent when the temperature is 62 degrees fahrenheit with a southwest wind of at least 16 MPH. Old-school baseball is practically extinct, as are complete games, bunting, hit and run, and nearly all fundamentals. My legendary collegiate coach, the incomparable Rod Dedeaux is no doubt, rolling over in his grave. No one stressed fundamentals more than Dedeaux, whose record of NCAA baseball championships at USC will never be challenged.

Recently, Diana and I reunited with Scott and his wife, Peg, at a celebrity golf tournament in Boothbay Harbor, Maine. We exchanged fond remembrances, some of which were actually true. At one time during dinner, Diana stated, "You guys sure like to embellish," to which I replied, "It's poetic license."

Which brings me to: Scott Russell is a terrific storyteller. "The Scorekeeper" is a perfect example of Scott's ability to effectively spin a yarn. I will admit that I find the most endearing character in this tome to be the eccentric southpaw hurler "Tim Barrett." I have absolutely no clue as to how Scott dreamed up this character, but imagine a major league pitcher winning exactly 17 games for three consecutive seasons! Seriously, what are the odds?

Oh, did I mention that I won that celebrity golf tournament in Boothbay Harbor? Playing against numerous former Red Sox, Bruins, and Patriots players, I shot a 73! And this during a year in which the Montreal Expos won the World Series.

Enjoy Scott Russell's "The Scorekeeper."

Sincerely,
Bill "Spaceman" Lee
Earth, 2019

A Letter from the Author

Faith and magic have guided me from the time I reached the age of reason. The age of reason, as it were, arrived considerably later in my life than it does for the majority of sentient humans. I will make no excuses: It's just that my frontal lobes took a bit longer to develop than most of my peers.

This latest work which you hold in your hands or perhaps on your computer screen is titled "The Scorekeeper." I did not originally intend it to be a play, as it is designated. I suppose it is part novel, part stage play. I believe it to be all magic, however. Even in my advanced state of age, I am a dreamer. Therefore, I acquire inspiration from countless sources, most of it from my fellow homo sapiens. My prior novel "Prophet's End" was inspired by my idol, Pete Hamill, an impossibly beautiful young woman named Jennifer Bricker and paid homage to First Responders. The character "Lauren Bartlett" in "The Scorekeeper" was inspired by a beautiful young woman I never actually met. Several years ago I saw this breathtaking beauty being wheeled into the Providence Performing Arts Center where a remake stage production of "Oklahoma" was appearing. Unlike "Lauren Bartlett," she was blonde, but I never introduced myself. As I watched the stage play I literally wrote "The

Scorekeeper" in my mind. I've never seen her return to the theater. I suspect she'll never know.

The character "Jen Volkov" is also based on an actual person, although she'll also never know. Unlike Jen Volkov, she spoke with an Irish brogue, waddled like a duck, quoted Shakespeare, Keats, Tennyson and Brendan Behan and drank Bushmill's Whiskey as if it were water. Then she waddled away, breaking a young man's heart, a heart that has since mended.

The character "Tim Barrett" is based directly on my old and dear friend, "Bill "Spaceman" Lee, the eccentric, erudite, controversial former pitcher and a former gubernatorial (don't you love that word?) candidate of the great state of Vermont. Recently I asked Bill if he would write a blurb for "The Scorekeeper," but he insisted on writing the entire preface. In October of 2019, Peg, my long suffering bride of 35 years and I reunited with "The Spaceman" at a celebrity golf tournament in beautiful Boothbay Harbor, Maine and despite the fact that we hadn't seen each other for a considerable time, Bill and I regaled each other with tales of the past, some of which were actually true! Remember the line from John Ford's epic "The Man Who Shot Liberty Valance," the one that goes, "When legend becomes fact, print the legend."

For the record, the best biography I've ever read, sports or otherwise, was penned by the inimitable Jane Leavy and it is titled "The Big Fella." Ms. Leavy's tome which took nearly a decade to research is the definitive story of the life of the immortal Babe Ruth. "The Big Fella" dispels all of the erroneous myths and false "truths" in regard to the life of the singular most famous athlete in American history. However, "The Scorekeeper" begins with Babe Ruth's iconic "called shot" and may conceivably be the only "fact" that Jane Leavy overlooked.

Here's hoping that you enjoy "The Scorekeeper." It was written with YOU in mind. In the eternal words of Tom Robbins, "Disbelief in magic can force a poor soul into believing in government and business."

> Be Well
> Scott D. Russell
> N. Attleboro, Massachusetts

The Scorekeeper

Prelap: the sound of chicadees through an open window.

Int: a hotel room in NORTH CHICAGO–OCT. 1, 1932

At daybreak, Stuart Applewhite (35) is awakened by the sounds of black-capped chickadees. He shivers as he approaches an open window. He closes the window and laughs as he recalls his dear friend, "Babe" Ruth's instructions from the night before.

STUART [*V.O.*]: "Go on and get some rest, Stu. You may have to do some serious writing tomorrow afternoon!"
Crazy bastard, I've been baby- sitting "The Babe" my entire adult life. Geez, when I left the North Chicago Speakeasy at midnight, it looked as if Babe was just getting warmed up. A babe to each side of him and a bottle of gin on the bar!

STUART: [*Stuart suddenly wheels around from the window and speaks aloud.*] The pen! Yes, the pen!
[*Stuart walks to his travel bag and removes a glistening pen from an envelope and holds it aloft. He revolves it slowly in his fingers.*] Magnificent! Magnificent!

[*After breakfast in the dining room of the hotel, Stuart takes a walk around the Chicago lakefront.*]

STUART: I wonder what condition "The Babe" will arrive in this afternoon.

[Fade to black.]

Fade in

Superimpose: Wrigley Field, Chicago–game three, 1932 world series–afternoon.

BABE RUTH (37) stands in the batter's box looking the worse for wear. The Chicago Cubs dugout, sensing that Babe may have done too much carousing, hurls insults at every opportunity.

CUBS PLAYER #1: Hey, Babe, you need an ice pack, you old geezer?

CUBS PLAYER #2: Was that an orangutan I saw you with last night? That was the ugliest broad I've ever seen!

[Charlie Root (33), the hard-throwing Chicago Cubs right- hander, peers in for a sign from his catcher. Root rears back and delivers a letter high fast-ball. Babe Ruth watches the ball go by.]

UMPIRE: Strike one!

[The insults and derogatory invective continue from the Cubs dugout. Suddenly Babe Ruth smiles at his antagonists and points towards the center field bleachers. Babe Ruth was calling his shot! Charlie Root takes a deep breath on the mound and laughs before firing another fast-ball, which Babe once more looks at.]

UMPIRE: *[bellowing]* Strike Two!

[Babe Ruth backs out of the batter's box, seemingly oblivious to the cat- calls freely emanating from the Cubs dugout. Babe then glances over to the seats beyond the Cubs dugout. Ruth winces, as if experiencing a se-

4

vere migraine, squints and then makes eye contact with a young gentle-man in a brown fedora, his friend, Stuart Applewhite. Applewhite smiles and holds up a shiny object in his right hand, a pen. Stuart looks down at his scorecard and appears to make a notation.

He then looks up and nods affirmatively. Babe Ruth turns and once more faces the Cubs pitcher, Charlie Root. Babe once more points to the nether regions of the stadium, the far away bleachers in center field. Charlie Root laughs, takes a deep breath and once more fires a high fast-ball.

The crack of the bat is heard throughout the far reaches of the stadium. Everyone looks on in awe as the ball sails majestically towards the very same bleachers that Babe Ruth had pointed to. The home run lands 460 feet away, beyond the flagpole! Babe Ruth had called his shot!]

[*Fade to black.*]

Fade in:

Ext: the campus of The University of Rhode Island–morning

Superimpose: Bill Beck Field, U.R.I., June 2001

A mobile news truck sits outside of Bill Beck Field, the home park of the University of Rhode Island Rams on the University of Rhode Island's campus. Inside the stadium, seated in front of a microphone are the newscaster, BRENDA CARVALHO (36) and young pitcher, NED BARTLETT (22). Brenda signals to the cameraman that the interview is about to commence.

BRENDA: We are here at Bill Beck Field on the campus of the University of Rhode Island. This field was constructed in 1966, but never before in its history has so much excitement surrounded the events, the baseball games which take place here. And we are sitting here with the reason for this phenomenon, the left-handed pitcher for the Rams, Ned Bartlett. First of all, Ned, thanks for joining us.

NED: My pleasure.

BRENDA: Ned, Bill Beck Field seats 1000, but never before this year has it consistently been filled to capacity. Although U.R.I is a Division 1 Atlantic Conference school, I'm sure you're aware that you're the reason for this sudden interest. How do you feel about bringing this attention to U.R.I?

NED: [*sheepishly*] To be truthful, a bit uneasy. Although I'm pleased that the U.R.I baseball program is receiving notoriety, I also feel a bit uncomfortable with the personal acclaim. Baseball is a team sport, and I feel that much of this fixation is detracting from the efforts of my teammates. I fear that I can easily become a distraction.

BRENDA: Well, Ned, like it or not, you've become an overnight celebrity.

Let's face it, by pitching two consecutive no-hitters and coming within one out of a third, is a feat formerly unheard of in collegiate or professional baseball. That, and of course, as "Sports Illustrated" described you, "A virtual unknown suddenly and unexpectedly thrust into the national limelight, Ned Bartlett, modest to a fault, also possesses Hollywood movie star looks, which, of course, add to his appeal." You have to admit, Ned, your accomplishments are chiefly responsible for your sudden acclaim.

NED: Don't get me wrong, I appreciate much of the attention and perhaps some of the adulation, especially from kids, however, I'm no different than I was before I achieved this "success." When I saw the "Sports Illustrated" caption beneath my photo, "Who is This Guy?", I began wondering exactly who I was, myself. One begins to wonder how much of the praise is disingenuous. I'm just a guy who loves to compete. I'm no different than anyone else.

BRENDA: Well, the same as everyone else with the exception that you've out- pitched every other collegiate star in the country. I just spoke to the Sports Information Director and he informed me that every major media outlet in the U.S. including ESPN has requested passes in order to see you pitch. Ned, to what do you attribute your sudden success as a pitcher?

NED: Finally, a baseball question! (laughing)

All, and I mean all of the credit should go to my pitching coach, Cameron Alexander. Cameron pitched professional baseball for 11 years, but never made it to the bigs.

However, he knows the game as thoroughly as anyone in it. At the end of my junior season, Cameron made suggestions that I adjust my grip, alter my release point as well as my arm slot and the results were astonishing. I gained 8-10 MPH on my fastball and my control and movement improved tenfold.

Hell, I wasn't even the best pitcher on the team, that was, and probably still is Bobby Burkett. I owe everything to Coach Alexander.

BRENDA: It's rumored that the Red Sox will make you their number one pick in the draft next month. How do you feel about that?

NED: I'm extremely flattered, of course. Hell, until my junior year I was still contemplating a career in either law enforcement or fire-fighting. Who knows, it still may happen.

BRENDA: Well, Ned, we really appreciate you taking the time so that our viewers will now have greater perspective for "Who is this guy?" Thank you, Ned, and the greatest of luck.

NED: Thanks for having me. Go Rams!

[*Superimpose: Federal Hill–Providence, R.I.,-June 2001*]

[*SUSAN PELLETIER (22), a lovely brunette is walking alongside her friend, ELLEN TRAVERS LOTUA (29). They had just emerged from an Italian restaurant where they had enjoyed lunch.*]

ELLEN: [*with obvious sincerity*] Sue, now, I fully understand why we haven't heard from you in a couple of weeks. You know that Tua and I are always here for you. You should have called. You know, To'Afa will be nine years old next week. You must come for his birthday party. He never shuts up about you, he says you're the best teacher in the world. I think he's got a crush on you!

SUSAN: Well, I've got a crush on him!
He's such a great and enthusiastic student. I wish I had a dozen more students like him.

ELLEN: Just remember that we're always here for you. You'll look back at all of this and laugh, Sue, you'll see.

SUSAN: [*her words belying her dejection*] I know, Ellen.

[*Susan suddenly springs to life.*] Seriously, you have no idea what you and Tua mean to me. You are always looking out for me and are so protective of me. I'm sorry to be such a downer, but Rick really caught me off guard, Ellen. I mean, we've been seeing each other steadily for over two years. I never saw this coming. I was blind- sided. I feel so foolish. We had actually discussed our future together.

ELLEN: It's his loss, sweetie. Trust me on this one. I know. You're special. Someone really lucky will win your heart, Susan.

SUSAN: To be honest, Ellen, I've lost a great deal of confidence.
I feel inadequate. Maybe it was my fault, Ellen. I've been poring over the last two years. What could I have done better?

ELLEN: [*somewhat sternly*] Stop thinking like that, Sue. It's not you. You're very attractive, you're sweet, you're nice and you're smart. You're the whole package.

[*Suddenly, Susan and Ellen are stopped in their tracks. Walking down the street towards them, are RICK (26) her recently estranged boyfriend with a shapely blonde (23) on his arm. They walk casually up the block, sharing laughter. Both Susan and Ellen duck into a doorway as to not be noticed. Quickly they pass.*]

SUSAN: [*sadly*] Two weeks ago he said he wanted some space.

ELLEN: Well, apparently there was much more than "space" involved. You got played, sweetheart. It's NOT your fault! It's his loss.

SUSAN: [*looking up the block and in frustration*] I mean, look at her!

ELLEN: I'd rather look at you. [*changing the subject*]

9

Hey, I heard you're going to Rachel Thomas's wedding this Saturday afternoon at the Coast Guard House. I think that Tua is tending bar.

SUSAN: Good, at least that way I'll have someone there to talk to.

ELLEN: [*sincerely*] Stop beating yourself up, Sue. He doesn't deserve an ounce of your self-pity. You are a terrific young woman. You will be fine.

[*The two young women embrace. There are tears welling in Sue's eyes.*]

SUSAN: I'll be all right.

ELLEN: You had better be. Hey, give me a smile. Call us any time, you know we adore you.

[*Susan smiles weakly and the two young ladies go in opposite directions.*]

[*Superimpose: The Coast Guard House-Narragansett, R.I.*]

[*A journalist from Rhode Island Weekly enters the restaurant to interview the bartender and bouncer, TUALO LOTUA (34), 6'7" and 320 pounds, the husband of Ellen Travers Lotua. He is escorted to the bar where Tualo begins preparation for another day on the job. The writer, ANTHONY FITZSIMMONS (55) is seated at the bar.*]

ANTHONY: So, how does a former All-American football player from the University of Utah who hails from America Samoa West, wind up tending bar in Narragansett, Rhode Island?

TUALO: Well, it's not as complicated as it may seem. While playing professional football for the San Diego Chargers for three years, I met a beautiful young lady, Ellen Travers, who would become my wife.

ANTHONY: So, your wife is from San Diego?

TUALO: [*laughing*] Actually, not. Ellen is from here, in Narragansett and she was on vacation. Well, as much as I loved Samoa, I also loved Ellen and the fact that she lived near the ocean did not exactly hurt our chances of settling here.

ANTHONY: I understand that Ellen is quite petite. You two must comprise quite a sight.

TUALO: That's for sure. Folks, especially our friends, often joke about the disparity. Strangers, not so much. I can appear quite fearsome!
[*laughs*] But I'm just a big kitty cat. It's a good thing the defensive linemen I played against never found that out!

ANTHONY: What can you tell me about the history of this extraordinary restaurant and its location.

TUALO: In the late 1800s, the U.S. Life Saving Service, now known as the U.S. Coast Guard, built this station of solid granite overlooking Narragansett Bay. The restaurant was established in the 1940s and we still feature locally harvested seafood. In 1979 it became renowned as a year-round favorite for diners. As you can see, we have a spectacular view of the Pier District on historic Narragansett Bay. We have customers from all over, local residents and tourists. And we also host spectacular weddings and receptions.

[*The manager of the restaurant had sat down near to both Tualo and Anthony at the beginning of the interview. Tualo turned to him and informed Anthony.*]

TUALO: This is the big Kahuna, JAMES PARKER. (51) This is the man to ask for details about the history of this establishment.

JAMES PARKER: [*smiling broadly*] Actually there is little else to add. Tualo acquitted himself quite well. I believe it's time to sample our menu.

[*Superimpose: The Coast Guard House–Narragansett, R.I.–Late June*]

[*Well-dressed wedding guests enter the Coast Guard House, many carrying gifts.*]

[*Int: The restaurant at The Coast Guard House.*]

[*Tualo is at his position at the bar which is in the center of the room as Susan enters. She approaches Tualo and they hug. Susan shortly thereafter takes a seat at "Table Four" as it appears on the card she picked up at the table which sat just outside the dining room. Susan is attending the wedding reception by herself. She fidgets and appears self-conscious. Tualo, knowing of her recent misfortune, watches her from behind the bar with the same concern he showed as he protected his quarterback on the playing field, however, sans the ferocity.*

Susan is seated at Table Four as other guests begin arriving. Shortly, five more people arrive at her table and brief and cordial introductions are made. After five minutes, Ned Bartlett, the suddenly famous young University of Rhode Island pitcher, enters the room. He is alone. The conversations in the room suddenly cease. There is a buzz.

Ned immediately senses the reaction, pauses, looks down at his card which reads, "Table Four," and attempting to appear as inconspicuous as possible, approaches the table. His seat winds up directly across from Susan Pelletier. As soon as Ned peers at Susan he is immediately smitten. There is just something about her.

For the next several minutes, the six other folks at the table completely fawn over Ned. All, that is except Susan, who merely observes as they ask banal, however, innocuous questions about his recent acclaim, baseball, the upcoming major league draft and anything in general. Ned, meanwhile, is dying to speak with Susan, who had caught his eye. Susan, meanwhile, had noticed that one seat at the table remained unoccupied, one with a place card which read, "Evelyn Higgins" in big block red letters. Finally, squirming, Ned managed to address Susan.]

NED: Hi, Susan. You're awfully quiet. What do you do?

[*Susan thinks to herself, "This guy is way out of my league. All the while Ned is thinking, "This girl is a cut above."*]

SUSAN: [*shyly*] I'm a schoolteacher.

[*Susan then places her hands on the table. Ned smiles when he sees no ring.*]

NED: What age group do you teach?

[*Susan's spirits brighten as she loves her students.*]

SUSAN: I'm a grade school teacher and I love my work. Children at that age have little or no inhibition. They're a delight to work with.

[*From his position at the bar, Tualo studies the conversation taking place. Although he cannot hear it, he notices that Susan's body language is excellent and that she appears to be at ease. The conversation between Ned and Susan lasts twenty minutes as they discuss everything from food preferences, music, motion pictures and television shows. The others at the table become aware that Ned and Susan have connected.*
Ned finally works up the courage to ask specific questions.]

NED: May I ask where you live, Susan?

SUSAN: Actually, I walked here. I live a short distance away in Narragansett.

[*Ned hesitates before asking.*]

NED: [*gulping*] Susan, if it alright with you, I would love to walk you home after the reception.

13

[*Susan's facial expression changes to one of uncertainty. Ned immediately becomes aware of that fact.*]

NED: I don't bite, honest. [*laughs*] I can assure you that my intentions are honorable.

SUSAN: [*biting her lip*] (I suppose that would be all right. [*pause*] Sure, why not?

[*Suddenly, the conversation at the table is interrupted as a lovely, blonde, EVELYN HIGGINS (24) arrives at the table. She is significantly late.*]

EVELYN: [*breathlessly*] Sorry, I'm late, folks. Hi, I'm Evelyn.

[*Ned greets the beautiful blonde with an overt friendliness, something which is entirely evident to Susan.*]

NED: Hi, Ev. Join the party!

[*Susan's shoulders sink perceptively although Ned doesn't notice. He is too busy smiling at Evelyn. However, from his position at the bar, Tualo Lotua is immediately aware of his friend, Susan's change in demeanor. Tualo shakes his head sadly.*]

As conversations continue at the table, Evelyn Higgins, the blonde, notices the look on Ned's face each time he peers at Susan, who continues light banter with Ned, but not with the same prior enthusiasm. Evelyn looks on with great interest, something which Tualo, at the bar, is also conscious of.]

[*As the festivities neared their conclusion, Ned turns to Susan.*]

NED Let me know when you're ready to leave. I'll escort you.

SUSAN: [*half-hearted*] Sure, I just want to visit the powder room, briefly.

[*Susan does not want Ned to know that she had not entirely made up her mind and first wanted to consult with her trusted friend, Tualo.*]

[*Susan walks towards the ladies room, however, pauses at the bar and has a brief discussion with Tualo, who peers over to where Ned sits at the table.*]

[*As Susan and Tualo converse, the young blonde, Evelyn Higgins, ceases her conversation with another couple and approaches Ned. She whispers in Ned's ear. Ned giggles. Ned, in turn, whispers in her ear. Evelyn giggles. This brief but telling exchange goes on for a few moments as both Susan and Tualo observe. Finally, Ned and the lovely blonde hug and as she begins to walk away, she stops suddenly, smiles and signals, "Call me."*]

[*Upon witnessing the entire conversation between Ned and the overly friendly blonde, Susan and Tualo nod their heads in agreement. Susan then heads for the ladies room.*]

[*Ned sits patiently at the table as the crowd disperses. Tualo stands at the bar, occasionally glancing at Ned as he washes glasses and cleans off the bar. Ned sits fidgeting in his seat. Twenty-five minutes elapse. At this point, only Ned and Tualo remain in the room other than an employee busily vacuuming the floor. Finally, Ned rises from his seat and approaches the huge Samoan.*]

TUALO: Are you looking for Susan?

NED: [*nervously*] Um, yes, in fact, I am.

TUALO: Sorry brother, she left.

NED: [*a bit confused*] She left?

[*Ned immediately seems almost disoriented. Tualo notes his obvious disappointment.*]

TUALO: Listen, brother, you seem like a nice guy. Maybe this will help.

[*Tualo reaches behind the bar for a note pad and a pen and begins to write. On the note is the name of a restaurant and lounge and the address. Upon completing the note, he slides the note to Ned and speaks.*]

TUALO: Listen, brother, the night is still young. I guarantee if you go to this bar, a good looking guy like you won't be waking up alone in the morning. Susan is not that kind of girl.

[*Ned's posture sinks. Ned slides the sheet of paper back at Tualo and replies with a hurt tone.*]

NED: You've really misread me. Hell, I was just attempting to work up enough courage to ask Susan for her phone number. I just wanted to walk her home. I don't even know her full name or where she lives.

TUALO: [*surprised*] You're not just looking to nail her?

[*Ned pauses thoughtfully before he responds.*]

NED: Honest, man, no. I really thought this could very well be the girl of my dreams. I never met anyone like her.

[*Tualo, normally a great judge of character, studies Ned and quickly realizes that he had indeed, misjudged Ned and now watches him sympathetically.*]

NED: [*dejected*] Now I'll never find her.

[*Tualo senses a genuine sincerity and after a few moments, puts his arm around Ned's shoulder.*]

TUALO: Hey, listen, brother. Maybe I can help. If you meet me here at 9:00 AM, I really think I can really help, okay?

[*Ned perks up a bit, not knowing what to think.*]

NED: [*hopeful*] I'll be here, if you're serious. I really like this girl... a lot.

TUALO: [*laughing*] Good, because if you hurt her, I'll be forced to kill you.

[*Ned laughs, but not nervously, concluding that Tualo was sincere.*]

[*Fade to black.*]

Fade in

Superimpose: The Coast Guard Restaurant–8:45 AM

Ext: The Coast Guard House

On a bright breezy morning, Ned arrives at the Coast Guard House. Filled with significant trepidation, Ned's mood lightens as he spots Tualo out front of the restaurant, waiting for him.

TUALO: [*broad smile*] Mahalo, my friend! Let's get this show on the road.

[*Tualo motions for Ned to climb aboard his Chevy Station Wagon parked at the curb.*]

TUALO: Your chariot awaits!

TUALO: [*Now seated, Tualo continues.*] Just tread lightly. Susan has been hurt recently and she's no doubt hesitant about jumping back into the singles scene.
[*pausing*] Sorry if I read you wrong, brother. I was just watching out for a good friend. She's a great teacher, too. I'm hoping she can find the guy she deserves. Who knows?
Maybe that's you.

[*Tualo pulls into Susan's driveway at 9:00 AM. Tualo climbs out of the vehicle and advises Ned.*]

TUALO: Good luck, brother. She's one tough little girl, but as I said, she's been burned recently. Being vulnerable and insecure is not an easy thing for Susan, but I've got good vibes about you.

[*Tualo rings the doorbell. Ned stands directly behind the towering Samoan football star, who is as wide as he is tall. Despite the fact that Ned is tall and athletic, Tualo's imposing stature completely obliterates Ned from view. As Susan opens the door, there could have been a Volkswagen behind Tualo, but Tualo is capable of blocking out the sun.*]

SUSAN: [*surprised to see Tualo*] Hi, Tua. What's up so early? Come on in. Is Ellen all right?

[*Tualo slowly steps aside which enables Susan to see Ned. Susan's voice drops a few octaves.*]

SUSAN: Hi, Ned. [*beat*] Why don't you guys come inside.

[*From the tone in Susan's voice, Ned perceives that Susan is not particularly thrilled to see him.*]

NED: [*apologetically*] I'm sorry, I realize your disappointment in seeing me. If possible, I'd just like a moment of your time. I promise not to bother you again.

SUSAN: [*somewhat embarrassed*] I'm not disappointed to see you, Ned. Really, I'm not. [*pause*] It's complicated. Listen, why don't you two come on in for a while.

TUALO: I'd love to Susan, but I've got to do some repair work at the restaurant. [*Tualo hesitates before continuing.*] Listen, Susan. I think we may have both misjudged Ned. After you left last night, we had a long talk.

This is a good man, Susan. Just hear him out and you might like what he has to say.

[*Tualo puts his arm around Ned.*]

TUALO: Hey, good luck, brother. If you need me, you know where to find me.

NED: Thanks, Tualo. I owe you, win or lose.

TUALO: Good.
[*laughs*] Because I'll collect, too!

[*Tualo walks towards his car, however turns and shouts to Ned.*]

TUALO: Keep your left hand up and protect yourself at all times!

SUSAN: [*giggling*] Gee, thanks, Tua. I can only imagine what you told Ned about me!

SUSAN: [*Susan's faint smile belies her inner turmoil.*] Have a seat, Ned. [Susan points to the sofa in the den.] Can I get you some coffee, tea or a cold drink?

NED: No, thank you. I'm not sure if I can keep anything down.

SUSAN: [*concerned*] Why, are you ill, Ned?

NED: No, Susan, I'm all right, just a bit tense. To be truthful, I feel as if I'm auditioning.

[*Susan senses the inference and reacts with compassion.*]

SUSAN: Ned, I'm truly sorry if I mislead you last night. I really had intended to have you walk me home....

[*Susan cuts off her response abruptly, as if attempting to choose the correct words.*]

NED: I really thought we had a connection. I really felt something, something strong.

SUSAN: Ned, to be entirely truthful, I felt the connection, too.

NED: Then why did you leave?

SUSAN: [*Susan ponders the question, thoughtfully.*] Ned, it's not you. Trust me, it's not you, I'm just going through some difficult changes right now. I'd rather not elaborate, but I really enjoyed your company last evening, too.

NED: Well, and I realize I'm taking a huge leap here, but to be entirely honest, I felt things I've never experienced before, much of it way beyond physical attraction, and trust me, you're a living doll, but I really thought that perhaps....

[*Ned halts in mid-sentence, as if fearful of continuing.*]

SUSAN: It's okay, say it. I won't be offended, I promise.

NED: [*cautiously*] I really thought that perhaps you were the girl of my dreams.

[*Susan is somewhat taken aback, however, inwardly pleased.*]

SUSAN: Ned, truthfully, I felt the same thing, but as I said, it's complicated.

NED: Susan, I've got all the time in the world. You're worth waiting for. I'll provide you with all the time and space you need. I'd just love to see you again.

SUSAN: [*Susan suddenly sits straight up in the love-seat she occupies.*]

Listen, Ned. The truth be known, I've been hurt in the recent past. I've lost a great deal of confidence. [*beat*] There, I said it. I just don't want to be hurt again. I don't think I could handle it. I mean, there you were last night, showering me with all kinds of attention. I was a bit overwhelmed. I'm not sure if I'm ready to compete for someone like you. Again, I really don't want to be hurt, and I certainly don't want to hurt you.

NED: [*Ned smiles slightly, believing there is a ray of hope.*]

Susan, honestly, I don't believe I'm capable of hurting someone like you. I really don't.

SUSAN: [*Susan briefly considers Ned's statement and becomes more animated.*]

All right, hear me out, Ned. As I said earlier, I really intended to have you walk me home last night, but then as I was getting ready to leave, and please don't get me wrong, you did absolutely nothing wrong, however, I turned and saw you having a very friendly conversation with that blonde seated at our table.

And I must reiterate that there is nothing wrong with a young, desirable handsome guy like you seeing as many young women as you can. But, I looked at her and she resembled a Hollywood actress. She was gorgeous, and I thought to myself, "How can I ever compete with a girl like that?" Then, multiply that girl with all the other girls you meet on a daily basis, and I just arrived at the reality that eventually, I'd be setting myself up to be hurt, once more.

[*Ned places his hand over his mouth to stifle a laugh. Ned thinks to himself, "So, that's it!"*]

NED: [*more comfortably*] Susan, may I have that drink, now? Perhaps a cold soda?

SUSAN: [*Susan, a bit confused at Ned's sudden more relaxed state, stands up and replies.*]

Of course, is Pepsi, all right?

[*Ned nods affirmatively and watches as Susan enters her kitchen. Susan returns, hands a can of Pepsi and a glass with ice to Ned.*]

NED: Thank you. God, you're lovely.

[*Susan, for the initial time since Ned and Tualo arrived at her doorstep, recalls that she had never even put on an ounce of makeup or combed her hair that morning.*]

SUSAN: [*embarrassed*] Lovely? I'm a disaster! When you arrived, I was hardly awake.

NED: [*laughing*] You're a disaster? If you're a "disaster," you're the most otherworldly beautiful catastrophe I've ever seen!

NED: [*Ned sits back on the sofa and searches for the correct words.*] Susan, that blonde last night….

SUSAN: [*Susan interrupts.*] You don't have to explain. It's natural, she was drop dead gorgeous. Seeing you whispering and giggling back and forth, made me realize my own shortcomings.

NED: [*laughing*] Tualo was right! You are one tough cookie! Please hear me out, okay?

SUSAN: [*Susan makes a zipping motion across her lips*]. All right, Ned, the floor is yours.

NED: [*sighing*] I never even stopped to think how the interaction with Evelyn, that "drop dead gorgeous Hollywood actress" would appear to you. I never gave it any thought. How stupid of me. You see, Evelyn and I have been whispering and giggling to each other since we were five

23

years-old. You see, Evelyn is my sister, and man is she going to absolutely love you! Hollywood actress!

[*Susan places one hand on her forehead and the other on her heart.*]

SUSAN: [*regaining her composure*] Ned, I am so sorry, I assumed....

NED: [*Ned interrupts Susan.*] There's absolutely nothing to apologize for. It never dawned on me how that conversation would look to anyone, especially you. Evelyn is married to my manager and agent, Brian Higgins.
Now, I must tell you what that whispered conversation consisted of.

[*Tears well in Susan's eyes, however, not tears of sadness.*]

SUSAN: By all means, I'm so sorry.

NED: Please don't be sorry. This is actually wonderful. This was my conversation with Evelyn, practically verbatim.

[*Fade out*]

Fade in

EVELYN: You really like this girl, don't you?

NED: [*giggling*] I think I'm in love!

EVELYN: [*giggling*] Well, go for it, I think she likes you. I've never seen you look this goofy.

NED: I don't know if I'm good enough.

EVELYN: [*laughing*] Just be yourself. You may be a dork, but you're a good dork!

[*Ned and Evelyn hug and embrace. Evelyn turns an walks towards the door. Evelyn wheels around and makes the motion, "Call me."*]

[*Susan sits stunned, wiping tears from her face.*]

[*Fade out.*]

Fade in

NED: So, Susan, will you go out with me?

[*Fade to black.*]

Fade in

Superimpose: The Coast Guard House–2002]

Ext: The steps outside The Coast Guard House

The bride, Susan Pelletier and the groom, Ned Bartlett, exit the Coast Guard House after the wedding reception.

Fade to black.

Fade in

Superimpose: Three years later

Int: Providence, R.I. Television News Studio—September 2005

On the 6:00 News, Reporter Brenda Carvalho sits at the news desk reporting the news.

BRENDA: Many of you may recall a story we reported on a little over four years ago, regarding a phenomenal young athlete, Ned Bartlett, a pitcher for the University of Rhode Island Rams. His meteoric and unlikely rise to fame resulted in a feel good story that you most likely recall.

Ned, an obscure and unheralded athlete, suddenly and unexpectedly became a virtually overpowering pitcher and graced the covers of national magazines and newspapers after hurling two consecutive no- hitters and coming within one out of a third.

Ned's career, as you may recall, came to an abrupt end due to a devastating arm injury.

However, Ned is still with us, living with his lovely wife, Susan, in Narragansett, and Ned was once more in the news and thankfully, good news despite what could have been a tragic incident.

You may recall the devastating fire at a nursing home at Rosewood Manor in Providence earlier today.

[*Show videos of firefighters battling the blaze.*]

During that blaze, Ned Bartlett was one of several firefighters that rushed to the scene and you may also recall seeing the video of one firefighter braving the elements and carrying out an elderly man to safety. Well, that firefighter was our own former U.R.I pitching star, Ned Bartlett! The elderly man, an octogenarian named STUART APPLEWHITE, JR. (84) is currently recovering at Rhode Island Hospital from slight smoke inhalation, however, is expected to make a full recovery. Ned Bartlett never made it to the major leagues, however, he is certainly a major league hero.

Fade out.

Fade in

Superimpose: Rhode Island Hospital-November 2005

Int: Nurses station Rhode Island Hospital

Ned Bartlett, firefighter, working out of Ladder Co. 8, Engine Co. 9, on Brook Street in Providence, walks down the corridor past the nurses station and continues down the hallway in order to see his friend, Stuart Applewhite, Jr. Ned is carrying several magazines and two books.

NURSE #1: That is one fine looking man!

NURSE #2: [*laughing*] Keep dreaming, girl, that ain't never going to happen!

NURSE #1: That's the sixth time he's visited that old fool this week alone! He keeps bringing him stuff, too.

NURSE #2: Hey, I guess he likes "The Wizard."

NURSE #1: Yeah, I wonder if "The Wizard" tells him all kinds of shit, too!

NURSE # 3: [*confused*] Why do you two call him "The Wizard?" He a magician or something?

NURSE #1: [*mocking*] Where you been, girl? Don't you ever hear all those B.S. stories he tells? He says his father was "Babe" Ruth's closest friend and he helped Ruth with magic. The old man is senile, I think. He's nice enough, but what a line of bull!

NURSE #2: Well, whatever bull he's telling the fireman, it must be working, 'cause he keeps coming back for more.

NURSE #1: Yeah, I wish he'd give me some of that magic, the fireman can put out my fire any time he wants!

[*All three women laugh.*]

NURSE #2: Too late, honey, he's got a wife and she's expecting shortly.

NURSE #1: You know something, though? This firefighter is a really good guy. This old fool, Stuart, doesn't have a friend in the world, no known relatives or nothin' You know something else? Ned's gonna find him an assisted living facility when he gets outta here.

NURSE # 3: What do they talk about, those two?

NURSE #2: Baseball, baseball and baseball!

[*The nurses laugh once more.*]

Fade to black.

Fade in

Prelap: A ringing telephone

Superimpose: Fire Station, Providence, R.I.–December 2005

Ned Bartlett is called to the telephone by another FIREFIGHTER (45)
Ned's shift is nearly over.

NED: [*speaking into phone*] Hello, yes, this is Ned.

NED: [*Ned listens intently before continuing.*] What?! I'll be right there. Thanks!

NED: [*Ned hangs up the receiver and speaks to another firefighter.*]
It's the nurses at the hospital. Old Stuart is fading quickly. He asked for me.

FIREFIGHTER: It's all right, Ned. Your shift is almost over, anyhow. We'll cover for you.

NED: Thanks, guys.

[*Ned quickly puts his coat on and rushes out of the fire station.*]

Fade out.

Fade in

Int: Rhode Island Hospital

Ned rushes past the Nurses Station towards old Stuart's room. A nurse stands vigil. Ned nods his head at her and she walks out of the room and stands just outside the door. Ned plainly sees that the old man is faring poorly. Ned walks over to Stuart's bedside and gently places Stuart's hand in his. Stuart immediately flutters his eyelids. Stuart grasps Ned's hand in his.

STUART: (*tired, raspy voice*] I never told you this, son, but my father was "Babe" Ruth's closest friend. My father on occasion actually made the Babe even greater than he already was.

NED: I wouldn't doubt that for a second. I was fascinated by your tales regarding Babe Ruth. I was so enthralled that I researched several because most historians missed many of the pertinent facts.

STUART: [*Stuart smiles and immediately winces, his time is short as is his breath.*] I'd tell you something about The Babe's "Called Shot," but you'd find it implausible, Ned.

NED: [*reassuringly*] I find nothing you say or have said, implausible, sir.

[*Stuart's response is nearly inaudible as he grows weaker. Ned leans closer to hear his old friend's words.*]

STUART: Thank you, young man, for not only saving my life, but for becoming my best and dearest friend in the very twilight of my life.

NED: It's been an honor, sir.

STUART: [*Stuart's voice is now merely a whisper and he struggles for air.*] I have a gift for you, son. It is something you must have. Please use it judiciously.

[*The old man then weakly points to the desk beside his bed. Ned opens the drawer and immediately spots a glistening pen which seems to gleam with every color of the rainbow.*]

NED: Why must I have it, Stuart? What do I use it for?

STUART: [*The old man gestures for Stuart to come closer. He grasps Ned's hand with all the remaining strength he can muster and speaks.*] I promise you'll know when to use it, son. Give it to your beautiful daughter. You'll know when the time is right.

NED: My wife, Susan, is expecting our first child shortly. We don't have a daughter as of yet.

[*Old Stuart Applewhite's grip loosens as he manages to utter weakly.*]

STUART: God bless you, son.

[*With that, Stuart Applewhite, Jr. closes his eyes, never to open them again.*]

Fade to black.

Fade in

Superimpose: Middlebury College, Middlebury, Vermont 2018

Int: A cafeteria on campus

AMY RANDONE (22) a Senior and language major, is seated at a table with a Junior, OKSANA PETSIKOV (21) a recent transfer student from The University of Illinois and a native of Kiev.

AMY: Wait until you meet my roommate, Jenny Volkov. You're going to love her. Everyone admires Jenny, she's a genius.

OKSANA: [*slight Russian accent*] Volkov? She sounds Russian, yes?

AMY: Yes, she's of Russian descent. Her mom and dad are from Uzbek-istan.
Her dad, Oleg, teaches at McGill University in Montreal. Jenny's going to be a great teacher.
Actually, she already is. If any of her classmates have a problem, she is the first one they consult. Even the professors adore her.

OKSANA: So, she is really nice, yes? I look forward to meeting her.

AMY: One thing, though. She's really eccentric. In a nice way. She's beautiful, too, a little brunette. Every guy at Middlebury is madly in love with her, but she hasn't found the right one, yet.

OKSANA: I'm sure she will, she's what, twenty-one, yes?

AMY: Yes, and one more thing. She's slightly cross-eyed, but when she gets excited, she becomes even more cross-eyed. It's adorable. She's also quite verbose, but not in a haughty manner.

OKSANA: Haughty? I'm sorry, my English is not that good, yes?

AMY: (*laughing*) Your English is perfect! Haughty would be arrogant, which Jenny is not. Her vocabulary is immense. It adds to her charm.
Half the time I have to carry a dictionary around with me in order to understand her. It's natural though, she's not showing off.
Even her professors are amazed.
And get this, Jenny's just as wordy in eight different languages!

OKSANA: Does she get excitable often?

AMY: [*laughing*] Yes, she's bat shit crazy! Oh, and one more thing. Although she's a genius, for some reason she absolutely loves baseball. She's sometimes preoccupied with it. Go figure. She even studies statistical reference books on baseball.

OKSANA: She must be fun to room with, yes?

AMY: [*laughing*] You have no idea! She has no enemies on this planet.
[pauses] Well, perhaps one. There's this pain in the ass baseball player on the Middlebury baseball team. His name is Jimmy Collins. He has the hots for Jenny, but she sees no reason for his existence. He's persistent, though, and a real pain. He's obstinate or perhaps just plain oblivious.

OKSANA: Perhaps he's ignorant, yes?

AMY: [*laughing*] Yes, that thought has occurred to me! Come to think of it, that's occurred to practically everyone Jimmy Collins meets.

Fade out.

Scene Thirteen

Fade in

Ext. A park near the campus.

Pert, vivacious JENNIFER VOLKOV (21) is walking through the park when she notices JIMMY COLLINS (22) approaching. She attempts to avoid him, to no avail.

JIMMY: [*crudely*] Hey, doll, how's about you and me gettin' it on?

JENNY: I would sooner enter into cohabitation with an orangutan in the final throes of tertiary syphilis.

JIMMY: You're funny, Jen!

JENNY: And you are not!

JIMMY: Aw, c'mon, Jen. Don't you know who I am? I'm the senior captain of the baseball team. I'm a great player, too. C'mon, give us a shot. You know you're hot for me.

JENNY: Listen, you ninny. I wouldn't be caught dead with you. Who did you blow to even get into this college? You're barely sentient.

JIMMY: I'm barely what?

JENNY: [*exasperated*] At second thought, I retract that statement. Listen, Collins, if you ever as much as speak to me again, I shall slice off your testicles and feed them to the piranhas in the Quechee Gorge!

JIMMY: [*bewildered*] There are piranhas in the Quechee Gorge?

[*Jenny, cross-eyed, walks away muttering to herself.*]

JIMMY: [*shouting*] Then why do you come out to watch me play every day?

JENNY: I'm watching the game, not you, you imbecile!

JIMMY: [*defiantly*]Yeah, well, I'm the best hitter in the league! I'm gonna be a major league star!

JENNY: You couldn't hit a curve ball if my grandmother, Marie, threw one to you. Run along now and do what little adolescent boys do. You know, drink a beer, scratch your crotch and just generally make yourself a nuisance to all of civilized mankind.

JIMMY: Hey, if you go out with me, I'll show you the best time you ever had, Jenny.

JENNY: I'm afraid I cannot take advantage of your largesse.

JIMMY: Yeah, I am large.

JENNY: [*Jenny sighs in exasperation.*] You spread joy everywhere, don't you? Listen, Collins, I mean it. If you continue to harass me, I'll be forced to remove your spleen!

JIMMY: Someday you'll be sorry for passing up on this great opportunity.

JENNY: I'm sure I'll be besot with grief. However, I'll attempt to abide.

[*Jenny, still cross-eyed, then walks away muttering.*]

Fade out.

Fade in

*Superimpose: northern Vermont, between Waitsfield and Waterbury–
hiking trail–Saturday morning 8:00 AM*

*Jenny Volkov exits from her car, secures and places two bottles of water
into her back-pack and takes a deep breath of the crisp clean air. Jenny
smiles, she loves the outdoors.*

*Jenny proceeds to hike for approximately forty-five minutes and then
turns her attention to a species of tiger lilies she is not familiar with.
There is no one else on the hiking trail. Jenny climbs up several feet
above the trail to get a closer look at the flowers. Suddenly, in the clear-
ing above her, a young black bear, extremely uncommon in the area,
emerges and appears almost as startled as Jenny.*

*Superimpose: It is often said of truly crazy people that they emit an aura
of invincibility not only to other humans, but to animals, as well.*

JENNY: [*breaking the silence*] I shan't be deterred by some silly little
canifom blocking my path.

[*The young bear stares seemingly incredulously at the petite Jenny
Volkov, who now becomes provoked.*]

JENNY: [*cross-eyed*] Proceed and do what adolescent little bears do.
Romp, eat some fresh berries, they'll provide fine nutrient for your growing
body.
[pause] I'll not be made sport of by some silly little honey bear. Run
along, now!

[*Jenny then points sternly in the direction of the woods. Incredibly, the young black bear lowers its head, emits a low growling noise, turns and saunters off. The day is about to become truly bizarre.*

As Jenny makes her way back down the path and nears the parking lot, there is a young couple from Brooklyn, New York, in the midst of a rather heated exchange. The couple is on vacation in an attempt to reconcile their contentious relationship. The young woman, ANGIE LoCASCIO (27) is furious. She scolds her boyfriend, TONY NARDICO (29).]

ANGIE: Tony, I saw you flirting with that waitress. Do you think I'm blind? I've had it with you!

TONY: I wasn't flirtin', Angie. You know I love you. Why would I ever flirt with anyone, babe? I got the most beautiful girl in the world.

ANGIE: Yeah, well, you better show it more often. The next time I catch you flirting with anyone, we're done, Tony. Understand? Finished, kaput, over!

TONY: Angie, sometimes you mistake being friendly and cordial as flirtin' I'm just a friendly guy.

ANGIE: [*sarcastically*] Yeah, well, if you were any more "friendly and cordial" to that waitress this morning, you'd have to get a room!

TONY: Babe, you know I love you. We've been together for what, four years?

ANGIE: Yeah, Tony, four years of putting up with you and still no ring.

TONY: You'll get your ring, Angie, you know that.

ANGIE: [*Angie stops, turns and points to the rest rooms located at the information booth.*]

Listen, I'm gonna visit the ladies room. Try to behave yourself for two minutes. You think you can do that, Tony?

[*Angie walks towards the rest rooms as Jenny emerges from the hiking trail and into the parking lot. Jenny is flailing her arms around aimlessly and muttering to herself. She is revisiting the encounter with the young black bear in her mind and her brush with mortality strikes her. The consequences and the possible repercussions of her ordeal suddenly overwhelm her. She staggers to where Tony is standing, her gait uncertain. She becomes light-headed.*]

[*Tony immediately sees Jenny struggling to maintain her balance.*]

TONY: [*concerned*] Are you all right, miss?

[*Jenny suddenly thrusts her arms up to her forehead.*]

JENNY: [*shouting*] Oh, my God, I came perilously within my demise. There was a black bear. I believe I'm going to faint!

[*Tony acts swiftly, and as Jenny was about to fall to the gravel pavement, he quickly and decisively prevents her fall and cradles her in his arms like a baby and holds her aloft. At that precise moment, Angie emerges from the rest room.*]

[*Angie stares incredulously at the sight. Jenny begins to flutter her eyelids and immediately recovers. Tony gingerly places Jenny on her feet.*]

JENNY: Thank you.

[*Jenny sauntered off as if nothing had happened.*]

ANGIE: [*infuriated*] Two minutes?! Two minutes?! Seriously?! Tony, we're through!

TONY: Angie, she fainted. There was this black bear.

[*Angie stands still incredulously staring at Tony.*]

ANGIE: [*irate*] She fainted?! A black bear?! Two minutes?! I suppose you saved her from the Martians on the spaceship, too!

[*Tony watches in disbelief, almost bemused, as Angie strides angrily out of the parking lot and down the road. A smile actually begins to crease Tony's lips. For once, he had told the truth, an absurd truth, but a valid if unbelievable actuality.*]

[*Angie LoCascio continues to walk indignantly down the road, far from her home in Brooklyn. She speaks aloud to herself.*]

ANGIE: How the hell am I going to get back to the hotel in Woodstock?

[*Angie reaches into her pocket and becomes aware that she has Tony's car keys.*]

ANGIE: [*laughing*] Good! The bastard is stuck back there!

ANGIE: [*thinking to herself*] I'll walk back, have him drop me off at the motel to get my stuff and I'll take a bus back to New York and rid myself of the SOB, for once and for all!

[*As Angie strides purposefully back to the entrance of the park, Jenny is seated at the information desk, explaining fully to a Park Ranger, what had transpired during her eventful hike. By the time, Angie LoCascio returns to the parking lot, Park Rangers are loading a small black bear onto the back of a truck. A crowd has gathered. Angie looks on dumbfounded as she sees Jenny standing near the men. Jenny Volkov appears concerned.*]

PARK RANGER: Stand back, Miss Volkov, although the bear is tranquilized, he can awake suddenly.

JENNY: What will become of the little fellow? He's actually a very sweet and amiable creature.

[*The Park Ranger smiles, as most men, he is practically overcome by Jenny Volkov's ebullience.*]

PARK RANGER: He'll be fine, ma'am. He'll be relocated, most likely to Baxter State Park in Northern Maine. I'm sure he'll remember you fondly.

[*Angie once more shakes her head in total incredulity and takes off in search of Tony. Angie smiles and nods at Jenny, who she recognized as she passes her.*]

[*Tony sits on the hood of his vehicle and practically recoils as Angie approaches. He is half expecting a full frontal assault He is taken aback as Angie smiles and reaches out to embrace him.*]

ANGIE: [*apologetically*]I'm sorry, honey, but your story really seemed off the wall.

TONY: Hey, babe, sometimes the truth is stranger than fiction.

ANGIE: Well, you have to admit, there you were, holding this really pretty girl in your arms and you're telling me about a black bear!
Hey, I saw the girl with the Park Rangers and they were loading the bear onto a truck. They tranquilized it.

[*At that precise moment, the attractive WAITRESS (32) that Angie accused Tony of flirting with earlier in the morning, passes by and calls out to Tony.*]

WAITRESS: Hey, Tony, don't forget to call me!

[*Angie's facial expression changes drastically. Tony shrugs his shoulders*]

TONY: Hey, I thought you were gone, Angie!

ANGIE: [*livid*] Yeah, well you were right! I am gone!

[*The waitress, hands on hips, stares at Tony.*]

WAITRESS: [*pointing at Angie*] Hey, you told me she was your sister!

[*Angie smacks Tony in the face. The waitress immediately follows suit and also smacks Tony in the face. Both Angie and the waitress then walk away angrily from Tony. The waitress then asks Angie.*]

WAITRESS: Do you need a lift, honey?

[*Angie nods her head affirmatively and the two young enraged women walk to the waitress's car.*]

TONY: [*shouting*] Hey! What about my car keys?

ANGIE: [*Angie keeps walking and with her back to Tony, she flips him off.*] I got your keys right here!

[*With that, Angie LoCascio, turns and flings the keys over a fence towards a path below the parking lot, where a family is walking alongside a stream. The keys strike a middle-aged man on the head. He cries out in pain.*]

[*Now, it gets even crazier. Jimmy Collins, Jenny's baseball playing nemesis and wannabe suitor, had overheard that Jenny was going to be hiking in these woods and had hoped for a "chance encounter." However, upon*] *seeing the two attractive women walking by him, the unrefined, obnoxious ballplayer alters his plans somewhat.*]

JIMMY: [*boldly*] Hello, there, you two lovely ladies!

ANGIE: Fuck off, bozo!

[*The waitress ups the ante by bopping Jimmy Collins over the head with her purse. Jimmy reacts with shock and while rubbing his head, scrambles back to his automobile in order to avoid additional abuse.*]

JIMMY: Geez, they have some hostile women around here!

[*Jennifer Volkov is a true force of nature. Unwittingly, in her decision to go hiking in the woods, she has an impact on the lives of many on this glorious Saturday morning. The collateral damage in her wake is extraordinary. The casualties include a couple from Brooklyn, an enraged waitress, an adolescent black bear, some poor guy just walking along a stream and a love struck, horny college ballplayer. Jennifer Volkov transcends mere metaphysics.*]

Fade to black.

Fade in

Superimpose: Three years later–Providence, R.I. March 2021

Int: Providence, R.I. television news studio–April 13, 2021

ROBERT SOUTHWORTH (38) the anchor of the 6:00 news, begins his broadcast.

ROBERT SOUTHWORTH: Well, folks, tomorrow is the day we've all been waiting for. After an absence of sixty-eight years, National League baseball is returning to New England! Despite the protestations of the Boston Red Sox, our neighbors from some forty miles to our north, major league baseball has come to Providence and we're experiencing Bays fever!

Although the Red Sox were diametrically opposed to another major league team infringing on their territory, the proponents for allowing Providence a team won out as major league owners voted nearly unanimously to provide the City of Providence this enormous honor.

Of course, the Bays, formerly the Tampa Rays, had to agree to shift to the National League in order to not clash directly with Boston's fan base.

We now go live to reporter CAROL HASTINGS (35) who is outside our magnificent new stadium. Carol, take it away.

CAROL: Ben Mondor Stadium, a testament to the resiliency of Providence, stands majestically behind me at the mouth of the Providence River and the head of Narragansett Bay. Our Bays, formerly the Rays of Tampa Bay, after years of less than adequate attendance in Florida, have relocated to our revitalized city, a city which less than a decade ago, was awash in debt and political corruption.

And I can assure you from walking around the streets of Providence, that the excitement level has reached a fever pitch and there isn't anyone I've met that is not eagerly anticipating tomorrow's home opener. Robert, back to you.

Fade out.

Fade in:

Int: Inside an apartment in Providence, Rhode Island

Jennifer Volkov, now 24, still astoundingly pert and zany, is in her living room in the apartment she shares with her former college roommate, Amy Randone. Jenny has earned her "Doctor of Modern Languages" and is entering her third year of teaching at prestigious, Brown University. Just as fortuitous, Amy Randone had secured a teaching job at Providence College. Jenny is still single.

AMY: Jen, I can't believe you're still a baseball freak. You're really going out there, tomorrow!

JENNY: I wouldn't miss it for the world. I've got to meet this Tim Barrett.

AMY: You've really got a thing for this young pitcher, Jen. I know he's hot, what else is the attraction?

JENNY: Have you seen the interviews? The guy is not only great looking, he's intelligent, hilarious, eccentric, erudite and zany. Did you see the interview he gave last evening? He equated the moral decay of society with the advent of the Designated Hitter rule in 1973. Then he immediately began conversing about the care and feeding of iguanas and discussed the arts and sciences, all within two minutes!

AMY: In other words, he's nuts, like you!

JENNY: Precisely, my love. I think I'm going to propose marriage to this guy. He has no idea how fortunate he is!

AMY: Listen, Jen, in an equitable and logical alternate universe, you two would hook up. However, this is the real world, Jen. Such a convergence is virtually impossible.

[*Amy Randone, who should have known better, was about to recall just how crazy her friend Jenny, really was.*]

Fade out.

Scene Seventeen

Fade in

Jenny & Amy's apartment, April 14, 2021–morning.

Amy Randone sits in a living room seat as Jenny emerges from her room.

JENNY: [*excited*] How do I look, Amy?

AMY: [*startled*] What? Oh, my God, is there something I should know? I thought you were going to see a baseball game this afternoon?

[*Jenny is wearing a white wedding dress, replete with a veil and a tiara adorning her pretty little head.*]

JENNY: I am indeed, going to the ballpark. I'm going to bag me a ball-player!

AMY: [*aghast*] You've taken this thing for Tim Barrett, too far, Jenny. You're a beautiful, intelligent and rational–
[*pause*] Well, sometimes rational person. Do not humiliate yourself, Jen. This is not a realistic quest!

JENNY: Relax, Amy. So, how do I look?

[*Amy takes a deep and almost resigned breath.*]

AMY: [*exasperated*] You look ravishing, dear. But you're bat shit crazy!

JENNY: Yes, of course, I am. However, I'm entirely resolute. Tim Barrett and I are soul mates.

AMY: Jenny, you know that I adore you, however, I fear that if there is a bona fide soul mate for you, he resides in a padded room at some mental facility with bars on the windows.

Fade out.

Fade in

Ext: The security gate at Ben Mondor Stadium–11:00 AM

Jenny arrives at the security gate. Many heads turn to see Jenny and not just because she is attractive. Standing alongside of the ticket taker at the entrance, a middle-aged security guard JAMES McNULTY (50) appears perplexed. The guard turns to his supervisor TOM RANDAZZO (44)

MCNULTY: Is that appropriate dress for the stadium? Do I allow her in and what about her sign?

[*In Jenny's hands, she grasps a placard which reads, "The Soon To Be Mrs. Tim Barrett."*]

[*Jenny glowers at both men as they read her sign. The two men peer intently at Jenny. There is a pregnant pause.*]

JENNY: [*softly, but sternly*] Listen closely, you knuckle scraping primates, it would behoove you to allow my entrance into these hallowed grounds. I shall not be denied my admission by two muscle bound quadrupeds. Any other decision on your part would incur my wrath. If you foolishly choose to bar me or my placard from entering, you'll quickly find that the halls of the Spanish Inquisition would be rendered mild in comparison to what fate awaits you.

[*Jenny, of course, immediately becomes cross-eyed, a fact which is duly noted by both security guards. This appears to more than slightly unnerve the two large men.*]

RANDAZZO: [*intimidated*] All right, all right, but don't create a distraction in there, or we'll be forced to eject you.

JENNY: [*demure*] Thank you, gentlemen, and in the spirit of fair play, I in turn shall not be forced to remove both your spleens. Have a nice day!

[*Jenny happily sauntered away to her seat beyond the first base dugout.*]

[*The security guards look at one another.*]

MCNULTY: Jesus, did you see her eyes?!

RANDAZZO: Yeah, and who wears a wedding dress to a ball game?!

MCNULTY: Those eyes, though! Jesus, I better check my pants, I think I've just been castrated!

RANDAZZO: You better call Kenny inside to keep an eye on her. Make sure she doesn't get anywhere near the dugouts.

[*Prior to the gala festivities which would honor the military and the introduction of various luminaries, little Jenny attempts to get closer to the Bays dugout, however, an usher, KENNY (55) previously warned of the possibility a "little nutcase," blocked her path.*]

KENNY: Sorry, miss, but no one is allowed to go down there without a ticket. I'm just following protocol.

[*Jenny accepts this edict because the man seems polite and sincere.*]

[*During the fourth inning, TIM BARRETT (26) for the initial time in his life, becomes aware of the existence of Jenny Volkov. After the third out is recorded in the top of the fourth inning, a roving cameraman searches for interesting subjects to project onto the huge "Jumbo-Tron" screen above the center field scoreboard. The image of Jenny in her gown, her veil in place, a tiara on her head, is then shown on the huge screen for everyone in the stadium to see. Jenny, unknown to Tim Barrett, has already created quite a ruckus and drawn significant interest from the fans in her section. Jenny, realizing she's being photographed, smiles broadly and holds her sign aloft.*]

[*LIONEL WIGGINS, (29) an African American and Tim's closest friend on the team and the offensive catalyst of the Bays is the first to notice the image on the huge screen.*]

LIONEL: Hey, Barrett, check out the board. I think you have an admirer!

[*Tim looks up at the huge screen, since he cannot see Jenny "live," as she sat sixteen rows directly behind the dugout. The southpaw Barrett views pretty Jenny curiously.*]

TIM: Holy crap! Is she nuts, or what? [*pause*] Kinda cute, though, don't you think, Wig?

LIONEL: I don't know, man, she looks dangerous.

TIM: We all need a little danger in our lives.

[*Tim then gets up, and approaches PETEY CORRIGAN (61) the team trainer and speaks briefly to him. Corrigan, in turn, goes down to the corner of the dugout, leans into the stands and speaks briefly with the usher, the one who had a quick, but friendly encounter with Jenny. The usher then leaves to speak with JIM CARRUTHERS (44) the sideline reporter for the Bays. By the sixth inning, Jim Carruthers arrives, microphone in hand, at Jenny's seat. Unknown to Jenny, Tim Barrett had relayed a message to find out who she was, how old she was, where she lived and any other pertinent information she might divulge. Tim views her exhibitionism as outrageous and self-deprecating, however, cannot shake the image of her immense cuteness.*]

[*Without being obvious, Jim Carruthers, an experienced media guru, manages to glean the desired information. The five- minute conversation with Jenny lasts even after the camera is turned off.*]

Fade out.

Fade in

Int: The Bays Clubhouse following the game

Jim Carruthers approaches Tim Barrett at his locker.

TIM: So, who is this girl?

CARRUTHERS: You're not going to believe any of it. She's not as in-sane as she appears, Tim. She's incredibly bright, her vocabulary is extensive and damn, she's cute!

TIM: [*laughing*] So, how old is she?

CARRUTHERS: She's twenty-three and you're really not going to be-lieve what she does!

TIM: Try me, I'm gullible.

CARRUTHERS: She's got a doctorate. She's a language professor at Brown University! She's a freaking Ivy League Professor!

TIM: No way!

CARRUTHERS: [*grinning*]
She's brilliant! Her name is Jenny Volkov, I believe. I know, I know, it was almost surreal speaking with her. I fully expected some sort of a deranged lunatic.
[*pause*] Well, perhaps she is a deranged loony, but she is super intelligent and a doll!

TIM: Did you find out where she lives?

CARRUTHERS: Barrett, are you seriously considering pursuing some sort of relationship with her?

[*Tim Barrett smiles, wondering about how his mom, an English professor would react to Jenny Volkov.*]

TIM: Hey, stranger things have happened. She was stalking me. Perhaps I'll stalk her.

CARRUTHERS: Ha! Yeah, believe it or not, I can see you two together, two incendiary devices, both awaiting detonation.

TIM: Hey, thanks, Carruthers. I owe you a dinner.

CARRUTHERS: [*laughing*] Don't thank me yet, Barrett. I heard this Jenny girl created some significant havoc when they nearly didn't allow her into the stadium with her wedding dress and placard. I suspect she's volatile.

TIM: Volatile can be a good thing, my friend. Thanks.

Fade out.

Fade in:

Ext: Outside of an apartment building in Providence–morning

Tim Barrett sits in his automobile across the street from Jenny and Amy's apartment building while awaiting Jenny's possible emergence and sipping a container of coffee.

TIM: [*aloud to himself*] Holy Christ, I cannot believe I'm actually doing this!

[*At slightly after 9:00 AM on Saturday morning, Jenny Volkov comes bounding out of the building. She is wearing a Tim Barrett jersey, blue jeans and sneakers. Tim quickly climbs out of his vehicle and strategically places himself in a position to block Jenny's path. Jenny, walks up the block, certainly not expecting to see the object of her affection. Jenny practically bumps into Tim. She is halted in her tracks. Jenny's cell phone rings. It's Amy, her roommate.*]

JENNY: Oh my God, Amy, it's him!

AMY: [*Amy's voice comes across loud and clear so that both Jenny and Tim can hear it.*] Him, who?

TIM: [*smiling broadly*] Yeah, him who?

[*At that precise moment, Tim's cell phone also rang. It's Tim's Mom, Aggie.*]

TIM: Hi, Mom!

AGGIE BARRETT: Hello, sweetheart, did I call too early?

[*Jenny stands transfixed just feet away from Tim as both are virtually stopped in their tracks.*]

TIM: No, it's not too early. In fact, I'm exploring Providence as we speak. Hey, Mom, I met someone, someone really special!

JENNY: [*distraught*] Oh my God, Amy, he's met someone! I'm too late!

AGGIE BARRETT: Do I hear a girl, Timothy?

TIM: [*staring directly at Jenny*] No, Mom, it's not a girl, but rather some horribly disfigured, mentally disturbed three hundred pound grotesque midget blocking my path.

JENNY: [*shocked*] How dare you, you heartless swine! I'm not obese and I'm not that short!

JENNY: [*Jenny pauses to examine her own body.*] I'm not grotesque, am I Amy? And I'm not fat!

AGGIE BARRETT: Is that her, Tim, the poor child I hear muttering?

TIM: Yes, Mom, and "it's" apparently mumbling in some unidentifiable guttural dialect.

JENNY: [outraged] It's English, you twit!

[*Tim's Mom then continues. She has an enormously great sense of humor which Tim not only tolerates, but encourages.*]

AGGIE BARRETT: I hope this girl is not anything like the last one "you met." I seem to recall that Bulgarian dwarf with the ankle fetish.

TIM: Mom, you promised never to bring that up! Besides, it was an elbow fetish and she wasn't a dwarf, she was a midget.

AGGIE BARRETT: I'm sorry, dear. Dwarf, midget, I get confused, something about one being proportionate, right sweetheart?

AMY: [*Amy, at the other end of Jenny's line is speechless. She finally speaks.*] Is that Barrett, the ballplayer?

JENNY: [*visibly upset*]Yes, Amy, and he's not at all what I thought. He's horrid, an abomination and perhaps the most vile and despicable creature I've ever encountered. He's heartless, a madman devoid of compassion and a villain of unimaginable proportion.
He appears to be nothing less than a cruel and evil despot. He is detestable! He has no doubt risen from the bowels of Hades! What was I thinking?!
[*pause*] And he's met someone!

[*Tim revels in the scene taking place. He is entirely smitten with the infuriated beauty standing directly in front of him.*]

TIM: [*feigning anger*] Will you please keep quiet, you hideously deformed little wench! I'm attempting to have a conversation with my mother!

JENNY: [*Jenny's eyes were now entirely crossed.*] How dare you address me in that manner?! Your recalcitrance and demeanor are appalling!

[*Tim suddenly diverts his eyes to Jenny's jersey.*]

TIM: [*feigning distaste*] You have the audacity of actually sporting my jersey?!

JENNY: [*cross-eyed and seething*] Do not change the paradigm, you insensitive misanthrope, you are the least salubrious being I've ever had the misfortune of coming in contact with!

[*Tim's Mom, Aggie practically chokes in delight. Amy's shocked silence at her end of the phone remains intact.*]

AGGIE BARRETT: Tim, sweetheart, that's her, isn't it? The girl you "met?" Did I hear right, did she actually use the words "paradigm, misanthrope and salubrious" in the same sentence?!"

TIM: [gleefully] Yes, Mom, isn't she magnificent? Plus she's adorable!

AGGIE BARRETT: Tim, do NOT let this girl out of your sight. Marry this girl!

[*Jenny begins to walk away angrily.*]

TIM: [*shouting authoritatively*] Come back here this instant, Jennifer Volkov!

[*Jenny comes to an abrupt halt, wheels around and confronts Tim.*]

JENNY: [*her face crimson with rage*] You are aware of my name?! You know my name?! What are you, some sort of a psychopathic, perverted degenerate stalker?!

TIM: Moi? Me, a stalker? Me?! I seem to recall this demented waif creating a spectacle at the ballpark, wearing a wedding dress and carrying this blasphemous placard!

[*At the other end of the phone lines, Amy sits silently with her mouth agape and Tim's Mom chuckles.*]

JENNY: Is there no depth to your depravity?! Do not demean, scorn or mock me, you misogynist half- wit! Go back to that girl you "found," your Bulgarian dwarf!

TIM: [*intentionally attempting to look cross-eyed*] She was a midget!

[*Suddenly, Tim's Mom's voice comes across the speaker of his cell phone. She is laughing hysterically.*]

AGGIE BARRETT: I'll pay for the wedding, Timothy. Do not let this one go!

JENNY: [resigned to her fate] So, where is this girlfriend of yours?

[*Tim suddenly bends at the waist, his 6'3" frame leans down to Jenny.*]

TIM: It's you, you little twerp!

[*With that, Tim bends even further down and grabs Jenny by the back of her head and kisses her. Jenny makes a half-hearted attempt at pushing him away, but succumbs and begins kissing Tim furiously. Jenny then immediately faints. Jenny had perfected the art of fainting, not an intentional talent, however, intrinsic.*]

[*By now a small crowd has gathered.*]

YOUNG MAN # 1: Hey, isn't that Tim Barrett, holding that girl?

YOUNG MAN # 2: Yeah, I think it is!

YOUNG MAN # 1: Jesus!

[*Amy's somewhat frantic voice comes across Jenny's cellphone.*]

AMY: Jenny?! Jenny?! What's going on? How come it's so silent?

[*Tim bends over and retrieves Jenny's cellphone which had fallen to the pavement. He is still holding Jenny in his arms.*]

TIM: Hi. You must be Amy. Jenny's fine, she just fainted. Say, are you going to be the bridesmaid when I marry Jenny?

[*There is silence at the other end of the line. Amy Randone, too, has fainted.*]

Fade to black.

Scene Twenty-one

Fade in

superimpose: Seven years later, Narragansett–April 3, 2028

I*nt: The home of Tim & Jenny (Volkov) Bartlett–morning*

Tim Bartlett enters the house, walks over to Jenny, hugs and kisses her and leads her to the sofa.

JENNY: [*great anticipation*] So, honey, do we commence packing?

TIM: Not yet, sweetheart, they just put Hal Chester on the 15 day Disabled List.

JENNY: [*sighs*] So, that amounts to a stay of execution.

TIM: You know, Jen, we've had a great run. I had a fine career, we made lots of money and have the two most wonderful kids on the planet. In many ways, I was actually looking forward to my unconditional release. Hell, the way I pitched this spring, I "earned" it!

JENNY: [*laughs*] So, you're ready for "civilian" life?

TIM: Yeah, and Hal Chester is a really good kid. He reminds me of myself when I broke in. Well, except that he's not insane! He's respectful, he's professional and he's going to be a helluva pitcher.

JENNY: So, you're really looking forward to living in Middlebury (Vermont) and rubbing elbows with the bovines?

TIM: Yeah, and I think that would be great to raise Jacqueline and little Timmy up there. Lots of space and fresh air.

JENNY: We're blessed, honey. And I've got that standing offer to teach at Middlebury. I'll miss Brown, but I always relished challenges.

TIM: Well, we'll have to put it off for at least until they release me. No complaints, they've been great to us.

JENNY: Hey, you won 17 games for three consecutive years before the arm issues.

JENNY: [*Jenny's facial expression changes drastically. Her mood suddenly becomes sedate.*] Have you spoken with, Rob? Has his disposition improved? Has your imminent release affected him?

TIM: Well, he's resigned to the fact that he and Phoebe are done. Hell, I believe he's more upset at my release than I am!

JENNY: I believe it entails more than your release, honey. Let's face it, he lost Phoebe to that womanizing, philandering, homophobic, racist boor. It's going to be difficult for poor Rob to be enthusiastic about rooting for the Bays this season.

TIM: Yeah, and to think, Rafner met Phoebe at a golf outing for the team.

JENNY: I recall how Rob would anticipate the commencement of the baseball season like most kids look forward to the arrival of Christmas. Nick ruined all of that.

TIM: And Nick is the best pitcher on the club, too.

JENNY: I actually believed Phoebe was a great deal more discerning than that. Nick Rafner is nothing more than a reprehensible, penurious, uncivilized bastard.

TIM: The woman is a clothing designer, too. I thought that required some common sense.

JENNY: Phoebe will rue the day she took up with that lout.

Fade out.

Fade in:

Superimpose: April 4, 2028–morning

Tim and Jenny hug ROB MORGAN (26) a handsome 6'0" tall, 180 lb. Travel Agent as he heads out of the door of their home.

TIM: I'll see you at the stadium, Rob. We'll get together afterwards.

JENNY: Dress warmly, it's not exactly spring like for the opener.

ROB: Yeah, cold weather and Nick Rafner is pitching. Lovely.

JENNY: Perhaps he'll be struck by a line drive and have to undergo surgery to remove his testicles.

TIM: That would be tantamount to brain surgery!

[*Everyone laughs.*]

Fade out.

Scene Twenty-three

Fade in

Ext: The streets of Providence, R.I.–morning of April 4, 2028

Rob Morgan is walking slowly towards Ben Mondor Stadium from his apartment on Olney and Hope Street in Providence. The overcast and cool temperatures cast an even deeper shroud over his already somber mood. He is depressed over the fact that he lost his girlfriend of three years to Nick Rafner, and that his dear friend, Tim Barrett's days with the ball club are seemingly coming to an end. As Rob nears the stadium, he uncharacteristically stops in front of a lounge named "Reardon's." Rob has never been to Reardon's before. There were very few patrons in the dimly lit lounge and none seated at the bar. Rob takes a seat on a stool at the bar.

ALVIN LACY (55) BARTENDER: What will you have, young man?

ROB: [*politely*] I'll have a Sam Adams, sir.

[*Rob is deep in thought about his recent misfortunes as the voice from his left startles him. Merely moments before there was no one to his left or right, but suddenly a man sat on the stool to his left. Rob thinks it strange that he heard no footsteps.*]

STRANGER: [*suddenly and unexpectedly*] Young man, there are much brighter days ahead. There's a wonderful treasure at the end of the rainbow. Things are about to change.

[*As the silence is broken, Rob feels a chill. Rob does not turn and face the man, who peripherally appears to be wearing a black trench coat with the collar turned up.*]

[*His hat is pulled down to the extent that it was nearly impossible to see his dark features in the dim light of the bar.*]

[*The combination of the dim lighting and his dark features provide Rob with an eerie feeling of discomfort.*]

ROB: [*thinking to himself*] How could this old fool possibly know anything about me?

STRANGER: [*The mysterious voice once more halts the brief silence.*] You probably consider me an old fool.

[*The sudden words startle Rob with their immediate and accurate observation.*]

STRANGER: [*softly*] Whatever you do, young man, please do not cancel your trip to the southwest. This will be a most memorable birthday for you.

[*Rob is now entirely spooked. The thoughts invading Rob's mind are arriving fast and furiously.*]

ROB: [*thinking to himself*] How the hell does this creepy stranger know that my twenty-seventh birthday is next Saturday? Hell, at least he got the southwest trip wrong!

[*Rob now responds to the annoying man seated to his left.*]

ROB: [*sternly*] I have no trip planned for the southwest, I can assure you!

[*The now extremely bothersome voice responds.*]

STRANGER: Oh, but yes you indeed will have a trip to the southwest on your birthday.

[*Rob once more feels a distinct chill, however before he can respond, the shadowy man places an object on the bar in front of Rob.*]

STRANGER: [*soothing tones*] Please, young man. Take this gift, but use it judiciously.

[*Rob now desperately wants to leave and realizes that stopping for a drink was a huge error. He does not want the conversation to go on any longer.*]

ROB: [*annoyed*] Look, sir, I don't know who you are or what you want and quite frankly you're giving me the willies, but....

[*Rob turns slightly to his left, however, just as mysteriously as the stranger appeared, he is now gone.*]

[*Rob studies the object the man had placed in front of him. It appears to be a brilliantly colored pen which gleams incredibly brightly, even in the gloomy light of the bar.*]

[*Rob arises from his stool, makes a mental note never to go to Reardon's again and walks towards the exit and pockets the pen. As Rob opens the door to the street, he once more shivers unexpectedly.*]

Fade out.

Fade in

Ext: Ben Mondor Stadium–opening day

Rob walks to his seat directly behind home plate. Suddenly Rob cringes as he realizes that Phoebe, his former girlfriend, would be seated with the players wives and girlfriends, the very same section he occupies, because he had Tim's passes. Rob is seated for a few minutes before PHOEBE RAINS (26) makes her eye-popping appearance.

[Phoebe, a slender and attractive redhead makes her entrance and several of the other women gasp. With the exception of Nick Rafner's dim-witted friend, the right-fielder, Earl Coakely, everyone dislikes Nick and all are partial to Rob. Phoebe arrives wearing a plaid pleated mini-skirt, thigh high grey socks and a revealing top, highly unusual apparel for the cold April day.]

Upon viewing Phoebe's arrival, Jenny leans over to PATRICIA WIGGINS (27) Lionel's very pretty African American wife and whispers.

JENNY: Lord, it's obvious the influence that cretin, Nick, has had on her. This girl has been transformed into a card-carrying libertine!

[Phoebe senses various unfriendly gazes and slinks into her seat, three rows directly in front of Rob, who is humiliated.]

[Rob, embarrassed, makes a concentrated effort to not make eye contact with Phoebe and stares down at his scorecard. The Bays win the game 9-3, and Nick Rafner, to his added displeasure, pitches a strong eight innings before Rob's buddy, Tim, is brought on to pitch an extremely ineffectual ninth inning in a mop up role. "Protecting" the insurmountable 9-

1 lead, Tim surrenders two runs in a forgettable performance. Tim's days are numbered as when young Hal Chester comes off the Disabled List in mid-month, Tim's career would be over.]

[*Rob, a serious baseball fan, scores each game meticulously and is staring down at his scorecard as the game ends, hoping that Phoebe would just walk on by on her way out. Rob keeps his head down.*]

PHOEBE: [*disingenuously*] Oh, hi Rob. I didn't notice you. You were so right about Nick! You said he'd be a great pitcher two years ago! Isn't he great?!

[*Before Rob can respond with an innocuous confirmation of the obvious, Phoebe blurts out.*]

PHOEBE: Oh, I almost forgot. Happy birthday!

PHOEBE: [*Phoebe bounds happily up the stairs.*] See you around!

[*Rob has indeed, entirely forgotten about his upcoming birthday.*]

Fade out.

Fade in:

Int: The home of Tim & Jenny–following afternoon.

TIM: That's bizarre. Geez, the guy just sat down next to you at the bar?

ROB: Yeah, I'm never going back to "Reardon's" again. The guy gave me the creeps!

JENNY: Well, he did say there were brighter days ahead. My intuition says he will be proven accurate.

TIM: How the hell did he know it was your birthday, Rob?

ROB: Truly weird, but he was also insistent that I had a southwestern trip planned for my birthday!
[*laughing*] Hell, he was almost argumentative! Man, what a weirdo. Oh, and don't forget about the pen, "Use it judiciously!"

Fade out.

Fade in

Int: Rob's apartment in Providence

Late Friday afternoon as he prepares to leave for the ballpark, Rob discovers an envelope in his sock drawer. Rob suddenly recalls, "The birthday gift!" In a three year tradition, Rob and Phoebe would exchange birthday gifts months ahead. Neither, according to the rules, was allowed to open the gift until the eve of the birthday. How odd, Rob thinks, that he discovered the envelope on the eve of his.

Rob has entirely forgotten that Phoebe had presented this gift eight months earlier, in happier times.

ROB: [*thinking aloud, sardonically*] Gee, what did she get me? A Dear John letter?

[*Rob carefully opens the envelope, half expecting to uncover a 3x5 autographed card of Nick Rafner. Instead, he pulls out two theatre tickets.*]

ROB: How lovely, two tickets to see Rodgers and Hammerstein's "Oklahoma" at the Providence Performing Arts Center!

[*Rob notes that the tickets are for the 2:00 PM Saturday Matinee Performance, on Rob's birthday.*]

Fade out.

Fade in

Superimpose: Gregg's restaurant in Warwick later that night

Rob, Tim and Jenny are seated at a table enjoying a snack after the game.
They are celebrating Rob's upcoming birthday.

ROB: So, what do you guys think? Isn't it weird I'd find the tickets to see "Oklahoma" at PPAC? Hey, I'm not going, would you like the tickets?

TIM: Thanks, we would have loved to, but remember there's a game tomorrow afternoon.

ROB: Oh, that's right, I did forget.

JENNY: [*Suddenly, Jenny, her wheels always in motion becomes animated and excited.*] Rob! Oklahoma on your birthday! Now you must attend!

ROB: [*bewildered*] I don't follow.

JENNY: [*cross-eyed*] Don't you see, Rob?
The odd gentleman you encountered at Reardon's warned against aborting your trip to the southwest. There exists no ambiguity here. Don't you see?
Oklahoma! Now you must go!

TIM: [*laughing*] Jen's right. It's a date with destiny. Oklahoma on your birthday! The southwest!

ROB: [*smiling*] You two are beginning to frighten me!

TIM: Good to see you in good spirits, Rob. This is an omen of sorts. What possibly do you have to lose?

ROB: Well, for one thing, my sanity.

[*Rob laughs as he considers the absurd coincidence.*]

Fade out.

Fade in

Int: Rob's apartment in Providence–Saturday morning

On the morning of his twenty-seventh birthday, Rob awakes and as he begins to dress, he notices the envelope with the theatre tickets, now on top of his dresser.

ROB: [aloud & sarcastically] Splendid!

[*Rob laughs as he recalled Jenny's parting words from the prior evening.*]

JENNY: No guts, no glory. Go!

[*As the morning draws late, Rob is restless despite having no intention of attending the show. His anxiety compels him to leave the apartment and at least walk past the theatre.*]

[*Therefore, he leaves the apartment at 12:45 PM and strides towards Weybosset Street where the theatre is located.*]

[*At 1:00 PM, Rob feels awkward. He sees a crowd milling about in front of the theatre and notes that the majority of the crowd is comprised of couples, young and old and a significant amount of young children. Rob continues to walk a full block beyond the theatre and has every intention of returning home, however, he suddenly turns and reverses direction.*]

[*Before he is even consciously aware of it, Rob presents a ticket to the ticket taker and is admitted to the outer lobby where he is handed a program for the show.*]

Fade out.

Fade in

int: Providence Performing Arts Center

Rob suddenly feels a distinct chill, very similar to the one he experienced while in the company of the mysterious stranger in the bar on opening day. Rob is quickly jolted back to reality.

ROB: [*thinking to himself*] Oh well, I always did enjoy the musical score of "Oklahoma."

[*As Rob stands in the lobby as the ushers prepare to open the doors to allow the patrons access to their respective seats, he notices an attractive middle-aged woman pushing a wheelchair towards the orchestra entrance. Rob cannot see the person in the wheelchair, despite standing no more than twenty feet away, the crowd blocks his line of sight.*]

ROB: [*thinking to himself*] What the hell is the matter with me? I never stare at people in wheelchairs!

[*Rob, literally, for some reason unknown to him, feels compelled to see the person in the wheelchair, despite his fully knowing that if he were in a wheelchair he'd be extremely self-conscious. However, some strong involuntary force has taken over.*]

[*As the lovely older woman pushes the wheelchair further towards the orchestra entrance, she suddenly turns the chair laterally. At once, Rob has an unobstructed view. Rob gasps.*]

[*In the wheelchair sits the most extraordinarily beautiful girl he had ever seen. Rob is dumbfounded as he thinks her beauty is incomprehensible. Rob stands breathless, his hand over his heart, although he is not cognizant of its placement.*]

[*Rob, bewildered and astonished, actually doubts what he is seeing is real. He cannot avert his eyes from the beautiful girl, who he estimates to be*

76

anywhere from 19 to 25 years- old. Rob continues to gape wide-eyed at her enormous and improbable beauty.]

[*The young lady has shoulder length incredibly straight brown hair, a black wool beret resting on her head and almost sorrowful brown eyes. Rob Morgan was blown away.*

[*Rob does not feel an ounce of pity or sorrow for her condition, only complete amazement at her beauty. Rob also notices that the young lady does not smile.*

ROB: [*thinking to himself*] Have I taken leave of my senses?! I'm in freaking love and I don't even know her! I'm a rational sensible human being. You've got to stop this, Rob!

However, Rob is smitten. He continues to stare at the wheelchair bound beauty.

The young woman in the wheelchair never even notices Rob's presence.

She is preoccupied as she removes her light tan gloves and hands them to the attractive older woman. She appears to be making an attempt to avoid eye contact with anyone. Although the young woman is not aware of Rob's constant vigilance, the older woman indeed, takes notice.

OLDER WOMAN: [*thinking to herself*] Good. There's no pity in his eyes, only curiosity.

The doors to the orchestra open and the wheelchair bound beauty is allowed to enter before the other patrons.

Rob watches as she is led to an aisle seat approximately halfway to the stage and is subsequently assisted by the older woman into her seat. Rob watches as the older women carefully lifts the stunning beauty onto her seat, the beautiful girl helping herself as she utilizes her arms, her lifeless limbs dangling limply.

The older woman, with the assistance of an usher, folds up the wheelchair and carries it towards the back of the theatre, eventually disappearing into the lobby. Still, Rob cannot take his eyes off of her.

As fate would have it, Rob's seat winds up being exactly three rows behind the young lady. Shortly thereafter, the older woman returns, places an afghan over the young lady's legs, a blanket gently over her shoulders and takes the seat next to her. The older woman suddenly turns and notices Rob's almost dumbfounded stare and smiles wanly at him although Rob is completely oblivious.

ROB: [*thinking to himself*] I'm intelligent! I'm rational! How can I possibly justify falling hopelessly in love with a total stranger in a wheelchair?! Ridiculous!

Rob does not feel lust for the girl, however, is sexually attracted, but not the raging hormones of a young adolescent. He sees an aura around her, an unmistakable glow.

The curtains part, the orchestra plays and "Oklahoma" is about to begin. Rob sits three rows behind the astounding, breathtaking beauty, head-over-heels in love and furiously attempting to invent a way to introduce himself to her.

LAUREN AMBER BARTLETT (24) the young lady in the wheelchair, is the daughter of Ned Bartlett, pitcher turned firefighter and her mother, SUSAN BARTLETT (49), the former Susan Pelletier.

Fade out.

Fade in

Superimpose: Twenty-four years earlier–Rhode Island Hospital- 2004

Int: Hospital room

Susan Bartlett is sitting in her bed as Ned Bartlett, her husband holds her hand. DR. WILFRED MAXWELL (52) speaks to the young couple.

DR. MAXWELL: [*hushed tones*] Your newborn daughter is a beautiful baby, however, she suffers from a rare genetic disorder. While I realize that this is not the news you desire to hear, I can assure you that Lauren is otherwise completely healthy.

SUSAN: [*tears welling in her eyes*] Are you certain she'll never be able to walk?

DR. MAXWELL: I'm afraid that fact is indeed, certain. There are no prior records of any of these babies becoming ambulatory. As I said, however, your baby is otherwise entirely healthy. She can live a full and productive life.

[*Ned continues to hold Susan's hand and leans over to kiss her.*]

NED: [*reassuringly*] Our baby girl is beautiful. She'll be fine and yes, we'll be fine.
Thank you, Doctor.

Fade out.

Fade in

Superimpose: Ogunquit Beach, Maine–Summer of 2013

LAUREN BARTLETT (9) is lying on a blanket on her ninth birthday, her under-developed legs covered by a blanket, to shield her from the stares and comments of other children. Lauren, an exceptional artist is painting the Oceanside, seagulls and the scenery, however, she longs to run and romp on the beach and swim with the other "normal" children.

As beautiful Lauren longingly watches the other children, her father, Ned, senses a look of sadness on his daughter's face. Ned plops down next to Lauren on the blanket.

NED: Hi, Angel. How are you doing?

LAUREN: [*attempting a smile*] I'm fine, dad.

NED: Listen, sweetheart. I have a special present for you, but it's very special, okay? Don't even tell Mom, it will be our secret, alright?

LAUREN: [*laughing*] I promise!

[*With that, Ned hands Lauren what looks to be a magnificent multi-colored pen. It seems to possess every color of the rainbow. As the sun glistens down on the small child and her gift, the colors seem to illuminate even more brightly.*]

[*Lauren rotates the pen in her fingers. She loves the feel of it and its aura.*]

[*Ned is pleased that Lauren seems thrilled.*]

NED: [*whispering in Lauren's ear*] It's magic, angel, use it judiciously.

LAUREN: [*Lauren laughs as only a nine year-old can.*] Daddy, that's such a big word, judiciously.

[*Lauren speaks the word slowly, phonetically, in a concentrated attempt to grasp its full meaning.*]

NED: Someday a handsome young prince will call on you. You will know him because he will also possess magic.

[*At night, while alone in her room, Lauren takes the "magic pen" and draws herself running and playing on the beach.*]

[*Lauren then falls asleep and experiences a vivid dream in which she is running and playing. She feels the sand beneath her and the shock of the cool water curls her toes.*]

[*Each time Lauren does this, she experiences the very same dream and is amazed as how authentic it feels.*]

Fade out.

Fade in

Superimpose: Ned Bartlett, firefighter-2015

Ext. A burning building, Providence

Firefighters are battling a huge blaze at a burning building in East Providence. Ned and his fellow firefighters have rescued all occupants in the three-story building, but Ned now notices that one of his partners, Alvin "Chip" Lacy, a veteran African American firefighter, is missing. Ned races into the burning building in order to save his compatriot, unaware that Alvin Lacy had escaped through a back entrance and was being treated for an injury.

Ned doesn't make it out alive. Ned's body is recovered by several other firefighters, but too late to save him. Susan Bartlett is now a widow and little Lauren, left without her beloved father.

Fade to black.

Fade in

Superimpose: A funeral parlor in Providence

Int: Ned Bartlett lies in wake

Little beautiful Lauren wheels herself up to her father's casket. Pulling herself up by her arms, Lauren slips the multi-colored pen into her father's suit pocket.

LAUREN: [*tears streaming down her face and devastated*] Draw yourself alive and well, Daddy. It will be our secret, alright?

[*Lauren chokes back tears.whispering*] Use it judiciously, Daddy.

[*From that day on, Lauren would no longer dream of running on the beach.*]

Fade out.

Fade in

Superimpose: April 2028-Providence Performing Arts Center

Rob remains dumbfounded by both Lauren's immense beauty and the unlikelihood that a seemingly rational human being could possibly fall hopelessly in love with a stranger in a wheelchair he hasn't even met.

Rob sits in his seat in the theater as thousands of thoughts enter his mind.

ROB: [*thinking to himself*] This is absurd. I don't know her name, I've never met her, what the hell am I thinking?!

Rob then suddenly conjures up the thought of what Jenny would think if he told her.

ROB : [*thinking to himself*] By the way, I'm hopelessly head over heels in love with a total stranger in a wheelchair. I have absolutely no idea who she is, if she's married or perhaps already has a boyfriend.
[*pause*] Ha, Jenny would think it's "normal!" Look at how she "courted" Tim!

Intermission finally arrives. Rob is nearly panic stricken. Rob's entire being reels with anticipation, excitement, apprehension, fear and even dread, running the full gamut of emotion.

Rob is not even conscious of the fact that he has walked down to Lauren's row. Many in the audience have left in order to stretch their legs or seek refreshments. Lauren's entire row is empty sans Lauren and her mother, Susan.

[*Rob seemed to be undergoing an out of body experience as he takes a seat to the left of both Lauren and her mom. It was as if he were on remote control.*]

ROB: [*startled to hear his own voice*] Hi, my name is Rob Morgan. Will you marry me?

[*Lauren is completely startled. She begins fumbling with the afghan draped over her legs, fervently hoping that the young man does not see her lifeless limbs. Susan Bartlett, however, looks at the young man she saw standing in the lobby looking longingly at her daughter, not leering but mesmerized and with a hand over his heart.*]

[*As Lauren turns, she sees young handsome Rob and attempts to compose herself. She quickly turns straight ahead as if to avoid eye contact.*]

LAUREN: [*jokingly*] Invariably, my suitors ask my name before proposing marriage, however, in this case I'll make an exception and I will marry you, but only if I'm permitted to wear white at my wedding.

[*Rob's heart flutters at her perfect voice, however, Lauren's heart is pounding, too.*]

Fade to black.

Fade in

Superimpose: Robert L. Carothers Library, U.R.I.-Three years earlier

Lauren sits in a chair at the library as several young male students approach her at various times, to ask her out. Her wheelchair is folded up and hidden from view and the young men are not aware of her condition.

However, in her Junior year, Bobby Simmons, a psychology major aware of her condition asks her out and she hesitantly accepts. They date several times until one day he calls to inform her he has to cram for an exam and therefore cancels their date for that evening.

Lauren enters a local movie theater that evening with her friend and fellow student, Angela Piccone.

Lauren is crushed and deeply hurt when Bobby walks in with a pretty redhead on his arm. Lauren, now 24, is still a virgin and extremely sensitive.

Fade to black.

Fade in

LAUREN: Invariably, my suitors ask my name before proposing marriage, however, in this case I'll make an exception and I will marry you, but only if I'm permitted to wear white at my wedding.

ROB: [*politely*] Seriously, may I ask your name?

LAUREN: [*laughing*] Do you mean you weren't serious when you proposed marriage?

ROB: [*laughing*] Of course, I was, however, I'll require your name on the marriage certificate.

LAUREN: Fair enough! My name is Lauren Bartlett and this is my mom, Susan.

[*Lauren continues to fumble with the afghan which covers her legs, not aware that Rob had seen them in the lobby. Susan, however, is entirely aware as she had noticed Rob in the lobby with the look of a lovesick puppy and with stars in his eyes as if in some sort of hypnotic trance.*]

ROB: Seriously, Lauren, I'd love to take you to dinner or the theatre. I'm hopeful you don't believe I'm being too forward, I can assure you that my intentions are honorable.

LAUREN: [*sweetly*] I'm sure they are, Rob.

ROB: [*deep breath*] May I have your telephone number?

[*The ten second pregnant pause seems like an eternity to Rob.*]

LAUREN: [*almost wistfully*] Why not give me yours, Rob?

[*Rob's heart sinks to his ankles. He immediately and accurately senses that Lauren has no intention of ever contacting him.*]

[*Rob writes his number down on the Center Stage Program and hands it to Lauren.*]

ROB: [*with disappointment*] Please call, Lauren.

[*Rob arises and walks back to his seat three rows behind Lauren and her mom. He is devastated.*]

[*Lauren's mom, Susan is taking the entire scene in. She is well aware that her daughter no doubt likes Rob a lot, but would never call. Susan is also aware that Rob is sincere and genuinely likes Lauren.*]

[*Susan believes that just as her friend, Tualo, had intervened years ago, she would have to summon up an equally effective method in which to assist her hesitant daughter.*]

[*Shortly thereafter, Susan scribbles their number on a slip of paper and plans to discreetly slip it to Rob after the show.*]

[*Rob returns to his seat shaken. The theatre lights flicker to indicate that Act two was about to begin.*]

[*Random thoughts race through Rob's mind. The thoughts come quickly and illogically.*]

ROB: [*thinking to himself*] I must see her again! Perhaps I can follow them when they leave the theatre.

[*Rob suddenly realizes the absurdity of his thoughts.*]

ROB: [*thinking to himself*] Follow them?! My God, I'm a common stalker, a perverted sicko!

I've reduced myself to stalking a young woman in a wheelchair!

[*Rob laughs nervously. Realizing his laugh was audible, he begins to clear his throat as to make it appear as if his laughter was merely a cough.*]

[*As the cast performed the songs from the Second Act, there is an overt sign of affection, however, it does not come from Lauren, but from her mother, Susan. Midway through the reprise of the song, "People Will Say We're In Love," Susan Bartlett swivels and smiled at Rob.*]

[*At the conclusion of the play, Rob is in an entirely confused state. Not knowing what to do, Rob walks out to the aisle in preparation to leave, but Susan pivots and beckons to Rob with her index finger. Rob approaches with much trepidation and caution. He has absolutely no idea what the older woman has in mind.*]

SUSAN: [*extending her right hand*] It was really nice meeting you, young man.

[*As Susan shakes hands with a startled Rob Morgan, she manages to slip a small piece of folded paper into his trembling hand.*]

ROB: [*nervously*] Take care, Lauren and Mrs. Bartlett.

LAUREN: [*sadly*] It was really nice meeting you, Rob.

[*Rob rushes out to the lobby and excitedly fumbles for the piece of paper, now in his pocket. He removes it, unfolds it and reads the words.*]

[*It reads, "Lauren, please call."*
A telephone number is written below.]

89

[*Rob's heart races as he floats down Weybosset street, his feet seemingly not touching the pavement. All the way home, Rob hummed, "People Will Say We're In Love."*]

[*Lauren, not aware that Rob knew she was wheelchair bound, sits in her seat for fifteen minutes after the show concludes. With the crowd now entirely exited into the street, Susan goes to the lobby to retrieve the wheelchair. She studies beautiful Lauren's face.*]

SUSAN: [*thinking to herself*] I have a good feeling about this young man.

[*At home, later that evening, Lauren, an accomplished artist, paints a portrait of Rob, although she intends for no one to ever see it. Lauren then cries herself to sleep.*]

Fade out.

Fade in

Int: Sunday morning-Tim & Jenny's home

Rob is greeted at the door by the couple's precocious daughter, JACQUELINE (6)

JACQUELINE: [*excitedly*] Hi, Uncle Rob!

[*Jacqueline gives Rob a huge hug. She is a miniature Jennifer Volkov. She has just returned from a brief disagreement with her younger brother, TIMMY (4)*]

JACQUELINE: I was forced to assert my authority moments ago, Uncle Rob. However, I made it known to Timmy that I was the supreme entity and informed the brazen upstart that I was to be treated accordingly.

[*Rob chuckles at the whirlwind and before he can even respond, he is pleased to see that she was not entirely an atypical child.*]

JACQUELINE: Well, I'll see you later, Uncle Rob, I've got to go potty!

[*Tim looks at his friend and shakes his head.*]

TIM: Poor Timmy. It won't be easy with a replica Jenny on his case.

JENNY: [*Jenny enters the room and studies Rob.*] What's up, Rob? You're absolutely gushing. You look downright refulgent!

ROB: [*grinning*] How could I not be, after speaking with Jacqueline?

JENNY: No, there's a significant change in your demeanor. Something wonderful occurred, has it not?

TIM: [*sensing something as well*] Yeah, Rob, what happened? Did Rafner get hit by a truck?

ROB: [*laughing*] Better than that, I'm in love!

JENNY: [*ecstatic*] Details! Details!

ROB: Well, her name is Lauren Bartlett.

[*Rob immediately ceases the revelations, since unknown to Tim and Jenny, by reporting her name, he has divulged everything he knows about her.*]

TIM: [*breaking the silence*] And?

[*Rob shrugs his shoulders as if to indicate there isn't anything else to disseminate. The thought suddenly occurs to him that he, too, knows absolutely nothing about the girl he had fallen hopelessly in love with.*]

JENNY: How and where did you meet?

ROB: I met her yesterday at PPAC.

JENNY: [*shrieking in joy*] I knew it! I knew it! You DID travel to the southwest!

ROB: The most beautiful girl in the universe, but it's not as shallow as mere looks. She's spiritual, it's palpable.

JENNY: [*feigning disappointment*] Are you saying she's more alluring than I?

[*Rob pauses, not sure how to proceed.*]

JENNY: [*roaring*] I'm being facetious. Relax, Tiger!

TIM: What does she do?

ROB: Um, I don't know.

JENNY: Does she enjoy baseball?

ROB: I'm not certain.

TIM: Well, when are you going out with her?

ROB: Actually, I haven't as yet asked her out, but I'm going to marry her!

[*Both Tim and Jenny stare at Rob in disbelief.*]

JENNY: [*concerned*] Please take heed, Rob. Remember, you've been hurt recently.

Fade out.

Fade in

Int: Rob's apartment-late–Sunday afternoon

Rob is pacing back and forth for several minutes, muttering to himself while attempting to work up the courage to dial Lauren's number.

ROB: [talking to himself] I'm a grown man. I'm twenty-seven years-old. I'm not intimidated by social interaction. What is wrong with me?!

After drawing a deep breath, Rob finally dials the phone. After three rings, Susan Bartlett answers at her home in Narragansett.

SUSAN: Hello?

ROB: Hello, Mrs. Bartlett. It's Rob Morgan, the fellow you met at the theatre yesterday afternoon. Is it possible to speak with Lauren?

SUSAN: [*warmly*] Of course, Rob, and I'm delighted you called, however, can you hold on for a few moments while I get Lauren? In fact, it might be a few moments, is that all right, Rob?

[*Rob thinks to himself that he'd wait several lifetimes if necessary and Susan's friendly voice puts him at ease.*]

ROB: Of course, Mrs. Bartlett, take your time.

SUSAN: Good, I'll go and get Lauren, then.

[*The delay in getting Lauren to the phone has absolutely nothing to do with logistics or in maneuvering her wheelchair, as Lauren can zoom around like a Nascar driver, but rather to convince her daughter to come to the phone.*]

SUSAN: [*Susan enters Lauren's room and calls out from the doorway.*] Lauren, it's for you.

LAUREN: Who is it, Mom?

SUSAN: It's that young man you met at the theatre yesterday, Rob.

[*Lauren stares at her mother.*]

LAUREN: [*aghast*] How did he get our number, Mom?

[*From the look on Susan's face, the one that made her late dad, Ned, fall in love with her, Lauren knows immediately that her Mom had pulled a fast one.*]

LAUREN: [*upset*] Mother, how could you?! I really liked this one, too, Mom. I never wanted him to see me like this? I just wanted to retain that one pleasant memory.

[*The expression on Susan's face suddenly morphs into total seriousness. Approaching Lauren, she takes Lauren's hands in hers and squeezes them gently.*]

SUSAN: [*compassionately*] Lauren, dear, you know I'd never do anything to hurt you, sweetheart.
He's seen you in your wheelchair. He saw you in the lobby yesterday, before the show. You didn't notice. He knows, Lauren, he knows.

LAUREN: [*Lauren's expression also changes drastically.*] Oh. Oh.

[*Still, Lauren wheels over to the telephone with significant trepidation. Upon hearing her voice, Rob's heart beats rapidly.*]

95

LAUREN: [softly] Hello?

[*Rob does not hesitate in getting to the subject. If he is to be denied, he feels he may as well make it as short and as painless as possible.*]

ROB: [*gulping*] I'd be honored if you would join me for dinner.

LAUREN: [*lilting*] Okay, but we'll have to postpone the wedding for a few weeks, since my white gown is at the cleaners.

[*Rob is relieved at hearing Lauren's sharp wit and response.*]

[*Suddenly, however, Lauren's demeanor and voice immediately seem to change to one of uncertainty.*]

LAUREN: [*nearly inaudibly*] Um, Rob (beat) you are aware?

[*Lauren had stopped in mid-sentence.*]

ROBERT: [*excitedly*] Yes, of course. I'm borrowing my uncle's van. It's wheelchair accessible.

[*Rob does not see Lauren's beautiful smile over the phone, however, he can sense it.*]

[*Rob and Lauren agree on a date for the following Saturday evening. Rob and Lauren sleep very little following their conversation, however, both wake up beaming.*]

Fade out.

Scene Thirty-nine

Fade in

Int: Ben Mondor Stadium–the following Friday

All week long, Rob preoccupies himself with his date with Lauren. He has made uncharacteristic errors at work and is a nervous wreck.

Before leaving for the game on Friday evening, Rob turns the channel to the 6:00 PM News and views the sportscast.

SPORTSCASTER: Despite all of the excitement surrounding our Providence Bays, it is somewhat tempered by the news regarding our popular veteran ace, Tim Barrett. Barrett, who won 17 games for three consecutive seasons just a mere few years ago, has been on a downward spiral since and his days as a Providence player are rumored to be nearing an end.

Barrett's release is apparently imminent, as he has not appeared in a game since a less than impressive performance early last week and it has been reported that as soon as young Hal Chester comes off of the Disabled List in a day or two, Tim Barrett, one of the most beloved players in team history, will be released. No matter what occurs, Tim Barrett, always know that you'll always remain a Providence Bay!

[Rob turns off the television and dons a sport jacket. The day is unusually warm for a mid-April. As excited as he is for his date with Lauren tomorrow evening, his mood is tempered by his friend's impending release. Rob leaves his apartment and arrives at Ben Mondor Stadium in a somewhat subdued mood.]

[Rob takes his customary seat directly behind home plate and is his custom, prepares to score the game in detail. As he lay his spiral notebook

across his lap to record the starting lineups, he immediately realizes he has left his pens at home in his desk.]

ROB: [*thinking to himself*] Damn! I never forget them!

[*However, his date with Lauren has rendered him discombobulated. Reaching into his coat pocket, Rob's fingers come across a pen.*]

ROB: Ah, I'm in luck!

[*Rob then removes a brilliantly colored pen and at once recalled its origin and the unusual man at "Reardon's" who had presented it to him.*]

ROB: [*laughing to himself as he recalls*] Ha! "Use it judiciously!"

[*As Rob fingers the pen, he feels a sudden chill, a very unusual occurrence on the unseasonably warm evening. Rob glances down at the pen in dismay.*]

ROB: Where is the point?

[*Rob's consideration is not meant metaphorically, but literally.*]

ROB: Where the hell is the point?

[*As Rob revolves the glistening pen in his hands, he does not locate a button to press or retract. He now believes that the pen is merely decorative and therefore serves no actual purpose. Rob cannot even locate any possible place where a cartridge would fit.*]

ROB: [*muttering to himself*] The darned thing is inkless. Well, it certainly made a great conversation piece!

[*Rob laughs at his dilemma, however, as he begins to place the pen back into his pocket, he hears an audible "click." Once more, Rob peers at the pen. He now notices a point protruding from the tip.*]

ROB: [*thinking to himself*] This is too weird. Oh well, I hope the darned thing writes.

[*Rob begins to write the lineups down on his scorecard. The pen indeed, writes!*]

[*Jenny, feeling a bit downcast over Tim's imminent release is not attending the game, however, had invited Rob to their "going away party" after the game.*]

[*As his former girlfriend, Phoebe Rains enters, Rob attempts not to make eye contact with her. Phoebe is dressed more professionally this evening. Phoebe's beau, the nefarious Nick Rafner is the starting pitcher.*]

[*The first three innings go by quickly, Rafner easily mowing down the opposition. The team builds a two run lead for Rafner. It appeared as if the overpowering Rafner was on cruise control. Rob's buddy, Tim Barrett, is out in the bullpen, shaking hands and exchanging sincere well wishes with his soon to be former comrades.*]

[*In the top of the fourth inning, Rafner retires the first batter on a routine ground ball to slick fielding shortstop, Eddy Rodriguez, as Rob enters a common 6-3 on his scorecard. The following batter walks as Rob records that entry. Then, one of the most, if not the most bizarre play in baseball history took place*].

[*The following hitter lines a base hit to right-center field. It appeared that the runner on first base would score easily, but Les Cameron, the Bays center fielder cuts off the ball and uncorks an unbelievable throw to nail him at home plate. The catcher, Danny Gonzalves, now notices that the hitter is now stranded between second and third base and an improbable rundown ensues. Gonsalves threw to the second baseman who in turn, runs the base-runner towards third and it quickly evolves into an episode from "Keystone Cops." Much to the delight of the sold out crowd, each and every one of the Bays players gets involved in the rundown.*]

[*The play incredibly results in an incredible 8-2-4-5-6-1-2-9- 2-7-5-6-3 double play! None of the writers in the press box had ever witnessed or even heard of a rundown play involving all infielders, all outfielders, and both the pitcher and catcher.*]

[*Media members immediately contact the Elias Sports Bureau and are informed that the play was literally the first of its kind in major or minor league history! The fans stand and roar for several minutes after the Bays run off the field.*]

[*They are witnessing history.*]

[*After recording his entry of this rare and literally unique play, Rob makes a discomforting discovery. He had neglected to flip his scorecard to the visitor's side in the top of the fourth inning and therefore, had transcribed the bizarre episode in the bottom of the fourth.*]

ROB: [*thinking to himself*] Oh, well. The entry is in ink.
I'll just have to chronicle the bottom half alongside of the erroneous entry as it unfolds.

[*The first batter of the inning, Lionel Wiggins, grounds out to short. Rob enters the 6-3 on his scorecard.*]

ROB: [*laughing*] Well, at least I don't have to change that one!

[*As the second hitter, Eddy Rodriguez walks, just as the second hitter of the opposing team had done in the top half of the inning, Rob snickers*].

ROB: [*laughing to himself*] I'll certainly not have an opportunity to retain the third entry!

[*No sooner that Rob denoted the absurd image of the virtually impossible occurring twice within moments, Booker Johnson, the third hitter, lines a pitch into the right-center field gap. The opposing center fielder performs an astounding stop of the ball, and prevents it from reaching the fence. He springs to his feet and makes a virtually impossible throw to home plate to nail a stunned Eddy Rodriguez, who had stumbled rounding third base. Then, as the crowd watches in total disbelief, another inconceivable rundown play ensues.*]

[*Incredibly, the scoring goes 8-2-4-5-6-1-2-7-5-6-3, the same exact play that had occurred in the top half of the inning!*]

[*As the fans howl in amazement in a chaotic scene, Rob sits staring incredulously at the gleaming pen in his right hand. Rob feels a frigid sensation in his veins and immediately recalls the shadowy stranger at the bar. "Use it judiciously."*]

[*The Providence Journal would report that an actuary estimated the odds of that play occurring once were "at least" a trillion to one. As for it happening twice in one inning, the odds were infinitely smaller, beyond even virtually possible.*]

[*Rob continues to stare at the pen in his hand, given to him by the mysterious stranger.*]

[*Rob allows the game to play out normally, literally fearful to jot anything down other than what actually occurs.*]

[*Suddenly, Rob recalls his friend, Tim Barrett, sitting out in the bullpen, most certainly spending his last moments in uniform. Rob stares once more at the pen. So, in the top of the sixth inning, with Nick Rafner in to-*]

tal command of a 2-0 lead, Rob summons up enough courage to make an entry on his scorecard.]

[Rob nervously pens "Barrett P. 0/3 6th." The entry indicates that Tim would enter the game before a batter was even retired in the top of the sixth, an extremely unlikely event since Nick Rafner had been overpowering and almost untouchable. Upon making the entry, Rob thinks.]

ROB: *[laughing]* There! That will render this pen a fraud!

[As Nick Rafner takes his warm-up pitches in preparation for the sixth inning, he suddenly doubles over in apparent discomfort on the mound. The manager, ED KEEFE (55) and trainer Petey Corrigan, rush onto the field, concerned about their ace hurler. Rafner has suddenly and unexpectedly fallen ill, with sudden chills and flu like symptoms.]

[Of course, no one is warming up in the bullpen. Keefe and Corrigan confer briefly with Rafner and the home plate umpire. Keefe turns and makes a motion to the bullpen with his left hand.]

[As the crowd recognizes home-town hero Tim Barrett trotting in from the bullpen, they rise as one and give him a tumultuous standing ovation that lasts through his warm-ups. If this indeed, was to be a farewell to Tim Barrett, it would be a memorable one.]

[At home, Jenny watches the game on television and sheds tears of joy as the large throng displays its love and admiration for a favorite.]

[Meanwhile, Rob stares incredulously at the gleaming pen in his now trembling hand. Rob is experiencing an Epiphany, as there is now indisputable and irrefutable evidence that this multi-colored pen was more than merely a writing instrument.]

[Tim Barrett had not pitched since his terrible outing on opening day. Normally a pitcher is afforded a mere eight warm-up tosses before an in-

ning, however, since Rafner had left with an "injury," Tim would be allowed as many throws as he deemed necessary.]

[*Rob shields his scorecard as inconspicuously as possible from others around him and writes a believable final four innings for his buddy, Tim, allowing an infield single and striking out three. Rob does not tinker with the offense of the Bays, who manage another run and emerge with a 3-0 victory.*]

[*Tim, enormously popular with his teammates, is mobbed after the final out is recorded. Jenny, tears streaming down her pretty face, wonders if she should begin to unpack suitcases.*]

[*Tim is interviewed after the game by veteran sideline reporter, Jim Carruthers.*]

JIM CARRUTHERS: Tim, you got this entire place pumped this evening. With rumors of your "demise," this must have felt really good.

TIM: To be truthful, Jim, Jenny and I began packing our bags earlier this week. We've had a really great run and we're more than prepared to begin our lives as "civilians." Time marches on and all of us are subjected to gravity. I'm a relatively young man, but an old pitcher.

[*The fans, many of whom have hung around after the remarkable game, listen in and cheer as the interview is being seen on the huge screen in center field.*]

JIM CARRUTHERS: Aren't these fans amazing? When you trotted in from the bullpen, this place was a din.

TIM: Stupendous. I literally had goose bumps. It gave me chills. The one thing Jenny and I will miss other than the great food on Federal Hill, are these wonderful fans.

Even as I struggled, these fans never failed to provide their love and support. Jenny and I were just speaking about that last night.

[*The fans roar once more.*]

JIM CARRUTHERS: So, do you feel rejuvenated? Four innings of one-hit shutout ball. Is Tim Barrett back?

TIM: Jim, as you are aware, this greatest of games will humble you. No, I don't feel rejuvenated. In fact, hell, I didn't think I had the stuff to get little leaguers out tonight. I missed my spots and fortunately, they didn't take advantage of my mistakes.

JIM CARRUTHERS: Well, Tim, I guess we can put off your retirement for at least a few days.

TIM: [*laughing*] Well, we'll see how it goes. That decision is the organization's and quite frankly, they've taken great care of Jenny, myself and the kids.

[*Tim, pauses, looks at the crowd still crowding around the dugout and concludes by waving his cap at the throng.*]

TIM: [*shouting to the crowd*] I love you guys!

[*Tim trots off into the dugout as more adulation and cheers follow.*]

[*Rob, sits behind home plate and seriously doubts his sanity. Rob was definitely not going to inform Tim and Jenny that it was a pen which resurrected his dormant career, certainly not now. Besides, Tim always preached about "the integrity of the game." Rob is both frightened by the pen and at the same time, strangely excited.*]

[*The bizarre events at the ballpark nearly cause Rob to not think of Lauren. That is, almost, however even while recording Tim's outs in advance, Rob thought he had seen Lauren's visage in the lights above the stadium.*]

Fade to black.

Fade in

Superimpose: Reardon's, Providence, R.I. –Saturday morning

Rob awakes on Saturday morning and at noon, pockets the multi- colored pen and sets forth to revisit the place he promised himself never to return to, "Reardon's," where the powerful "gift" was given to him by the tall, mysterious stranger.

P.O.V. We see Rob enter the establishment from behind the view of the bartender. Rob smiles as he is pleased to see the very same African American bartender that was on duty on the day of the home opener. Rob approaches the bar.

ROB: Good afternoon, sir. Do you recall seeing me?

[*The bartender sizes Rob up and retains a rather skeptical look. He seems to give the impression that he doesn't quite know what to make of Rob.*]

BARTENDER: [*cautiously*] Of course, you were in here two weeks ago, the day the Bays held their home opener. It was an unusually slow day and cold. There were very few customers.

[*Rob's hopes are buoyed by the fact the bartender remembered him.*]

ROB: [*excitedly*] Yes, I know. That's why I need your help, sir. My name is Rob Morgan. There was a gentleman wearing a trench coat, he appeared to be tall and thin, he had dark features and he was seated to my left at the bar. I could sure use your help in finding him. I'm hopeful you know who he is. Do you know him and does he come here often?

106

[*The bartender gives Rob a prolonged hard and suspicious look. He appears to be perplexed.*]

BARTENDER: Look, young man. I remember serving you one drink that day and if you asked for another, I would have cut you off.
You appeared to be sober, but there was no one, I can assure you, in either the stools to your left or right. They were unoccupied.

ROB: [*with sincerity*] But certainly, you must have seen him, sir.

[*Rob seems genuinely confused as he points to a stool.*]

ROB: He sat right there, sir.

BARTENDER: [*softly, but sternly*] No, young man, you were having a conversation with yourself. That is why I would have refused you another drink had you asked.
Again, there was no one on that bar stool.

[*Rob lowers his head in dismay.*]

BARTENDER: [*thoughtfully*] Are you sure you're all right, son?

[*Rob appears to be confused and shakes his head slowly*].

ROB: No, I'm not sure, sir. Look, I'm truly sorry if I caused you any concern. That was certainly not my intention.
[pause] Thank you for taking the time, sir.

[*Rob turns and walks towards the door, however, the bartender calls out to him. Rob pivots to face the bartender.*]

BARTENDER: Hey, Rob, you seem like an awfully nice fellow. You're welcome in here at any time.
[laughs] Just leave your invisible friend home!

ROB: [*laughing*] Thank you, sir. May I ask your name?

BARTENDER: Of course, son. My name is Alvin Lacy, but my friends call me "Chip." I'm a retired firefighter.

Fade out.

Fade in

Int: Susan and Lauren's home in Narragansett–Saturday morning

As unnerved as Rob was all week in anticipation of his date with Lauren, the young beauty seems just as anxious.

LAUREN: [*fidgeting*] Oh, Mom, what should I wear? Am I doing the right thing? What if he doesn't like me, Mom?

[*Susan smiles, fully aware that her 24 year-old daughter is not emotionally unlike most 16 year-old girls when considering the circumstances of her life, despite the fact that Lauren is extremely intelligent and talented.*]

SUSAN: You're lovely, dear. He already likes you a great deal, I can tell.

LAUREN: How can you tell, Mom?

SUSAN: [*smiling*] Because he looked at you the same way your father looked at me, Lauren. That's how I know.

Fade out.

Fade in:

Int: Susan And Lauren's home-Saturday evening

Rob rings the doorbell at 6:45 PM. He is fifteen minutes early.

As Rob waits for the door to open for what seems to him like an eternity, but in reality is a mere twenty seconds, he feels his knees wobble.

Susan answers the door, smiles warmly and leads Rob to a mahogany filled library. Rob notices several beautiful wildlife portraits hanging on the walls.

ROB: Wow, those paintings are extraordinary!

[*Susan, of course, is aware that Rob knows very little about her daughter.*]

SUSAN: Do you really like them?

[*Rob does not avert his eyes from one of the paintings, one which depicted a scene in the deep forest that featured a whitetail deer and its fawn, apparently during the fall season. The coloring and lighting indicated the time of day was near dusk.*]

ROB: They're wonderful! What incredible detail!

SUSAN: [*beaming proudly*] Well, perhaps Lauren will paint one for you.

ROB: [*astonished*] Lauren is the artist?! Please forgive me, I had no idea!

SUSAN: [*laughing*] There's nothing to apologize for, Rob. How could you possibly know that Lauren was an artist?

[*pausing*] Lauren exhibited a great talent for drawing as a young child. She eventually majored in art at U.R.I. Someone remarked that her style was reminiscent of a great wildlife artist named Terry Redlin.

ROB: [*laughing*] I can hardly draw a stick figure!

[*Susan arises from her seat.*]

SUSAN: Lauren should be down shortly. Can I get you some cold tonic or coffee?

ROB: No, thank you, ma'am, I'm fine.

[*Rob continues to gape in absolute wonder at Lauren's artwork.*]

SUSAN: Aren't you the gentleman, please call me Susan.

ROB: Yes, ma'am, I mean Susan.

[*Rob, resplendent in black pants, a nifty Irish knit white sweater and a gray sport coat, quickly notices Lauren wheel into the room. Lauren is a magnificent vision in a light amber dress that seems to accentuate her perfectly straight brown hair. A tan beret, once more, adorns her head. Rob sits in total awe at her astonishing beauty, once more falling deeper and more hopelessly in love.*]

ROB: Hi, Lauren.
[turns towards Susan] I promise to have Lauren home before midnight.

SUSAN: [*laughs loudly*] She's a grown woman, Rob. She won't turn into a pumpkin!

ROB: [*turning to Lauren*] Well, I'm glad you didn't stand me up. I was frightened you'd get cold feet.

[*Rob suddenly realizes his faux pas. He had not intended it as a joke.*]

LAUREN: [*chuckling and then laughing hysterically; Lauren clearly sees that Rob is humiliated.*] It's all right, Rob! It's okay!

[*Lauren pauses in an attempt to compose herself, however, she is still giggling. Susan loves the fact that she appears entirely at ease and comfortable.*]

ROB: [*embarrassed*] I didn't intend....

LAUREN: [*giggling*] Relax, Rob. You just made my day!

[*After hugging her mother, Susan wheels herself out to the van in the driveway. Rob is delighted as the ramp descends upon his electronic command. He is fearful of anything going awry during his initial date the young lady of his dreams.*]

[*Once they were in the vehicle, both stare straight ahead in order to avoid eye contact which belies the fact that both fervently wish they could gaze into each other's eyes.*]

[*Very few words are spoken on the ride to Hemenway's Restaurant in Providence, merely pleasantries regarding the weather and how they had enjoyed the musical score of "Oklahoma" the prior week, although in Rob's case, he is just making conversation, since he had been oblivious to anything the entire afternoon as he spent nearly the entire afternoon performance languidly peering at the back of Lauren's head.*]

[*Once seated in the restaurant at a lovely table overlooking the Providence River, Rob breaks the silence.*]

ROB: [*awkwardly*] So, do you like baseball?

[*Lauren is aware that Rob's overt shyness is affecting his senses and immediately becomes more at ease as she comes to the realization that Rob appears to be even more uptight than she.*]

LAUREN: [*eyes sparkling and smiling*] Oh, wonderful! First you ask for my hand in marriage and then immediately question if I enjoy baseball. I'm not certain where this relationship is headed.

[*Lauren's soft laugh and sparkling eyes in the soft candlelight of the restaurant, along with her light demeanor and pleasant disposition, immediately enable Rob to feel more comfortable.*]

[*Rob takes a deep breath and leans back in his seat, more relaxed.*]

ROB: Lauren, I'm not normally this tense, but you're so beautiful, I'm a bit intimidated.

LAUREN: [reassuringly] Relax, Rob, I really like you, honest.

[*For the balance of the evening, both Rob and Lauren bare their respective souls and share and discuss their likes, dislikes, quirks, idiosyncrasies and ideologies.*]

[*Rob inquires about Lauren's genius for painting and is amazed she possesses little ego.*]

[*Rob is entirely smitten, as is Lauren, who is cautiously optimistic despite her earlier "romantic" misfortune.*]

Fade out.

Fade in

Ext: outside of the Bartlett home later that evening

As they pull up to the house in Rob's van, Rob turns to Lauren.

ROB: [*timidly*] May I kiss you, Lauren?

LAUREN: Yes, I'd like that very much, Rob.

[*Lauren's exquisite kiss leaves Rob light-headed and Lauren, too, is positively affected.*]

[*As Rob and Lauren enter the house, Susan peers out from the kitchen.*]

SUSAN: Wow, you kids are home early. Is everything all right?

[*However, from the look on her daughter's face, Susan knows indeed, that everything is fine.*]

LAUREN: Everything is fine, Mom. I had a wonderful time and the food was great. Rob is terrific.
[*pause*] He swept me off my feet.

[*Lauren hesitates upon making the comment and peripherally and playfully glances at Rob to see his reaction.*]

ROB: [*uncertain*] Um....

[*Lauren giggles and tosses her hair. She got him good.*]

SUSAN: Rob, can you stay for coffee?

ROB: I don't want to impose. I'll stay if Lauren doesn't mind.

LAUREN: [*giggling*] Of course, I don't mind. I like you, remember, silly?

[*Rob, Lauren and Susan have a memorable conversation which lasts long into the night. As Lauren speaks of her dad, who she says would have really liked Rob, tears well in her eyes.*]

[*Rob considers it a revelation as he learns that Lauren's dad, Ned, had been a collegiate All-American baseball star before he became a firefighter.*]

[*At 12:15 AM, Rob notices the clock adjacent to one of Lauren's magnificent paintings, this one an eagle returning to its nest to feed its young.*]

ROB: Wow, I didn't realize what time it was. I apologize for keeping you up so late.

[*Rob is assured by both Susan and Lauren that it is not an inconvenience.*]

[*Rob arises in preparation to leave.*]

ROB: [*still not entirely confident*] May I see you again, Lauren?

LAUREN: [*playfully*] Let me think about it, Rob.

[*Upon seeing Rob's posture sink, Lauren immediately adds.*]

LAUREN: Of course, I'll see you, silly! Call me!

[*Lauren pivots in her wheelchair, practically doing "wheelies."*]

[*Rob, normally a great judge of people, is so blinded by his love for Lauren, that he is uncertain when she is teasing him. This, of course, would change.*]

[*Susan accompanies Rob to the door.*]

ROB: [*hushed tones*] Mrs. Bartlett, I mean, Susan. Your daughter is the most incredible human being I've ever met. I don't want to alarm or frighten you, but I already adore her.

SUSAN: [*warmly*] I can easily sense that, Rob. I also sense that you're the nicest young man she's ever dated and you are most certainly welcome in this house.

[*Rob Morgan, twenty-seven years old, feels as if he just survived his initial high school date. He doesn't even recall climbing into his van or driving home early that morning. For all he knows, he could have been flying.*]

[*That night, Lauren Amber Bartlett, dreams of a handsome young prince calling on her, a bygone dream she hadn't experienced since that horrible night thirteen years ago when her beloved fire fighting dad failed to return home from work.*]

Fade out.

Fade in

[*Int: Tim and Jenny's Home–Monday*]

[*Rob has not as yet dared inform Tim and Jenny that his mysterious gift, the pen, had salvaged his friend's career and as the season wore on, Rob limits the use of the seemingly magical pen to a minimum. There are two months of merely slight scoring modifications and nearly all to assist Tim in reviving his pitching career.*]

[*Tim, although throwing better, still cannot account for his "good luck." Loving baseball and not wishing to compromise the integrity of the game, Rob mostly uses the pen in order to extricate Tim out of some precarious situations, with an occasionally neatly turned 6-4-3, 4-6-3 or 5-4-3 double play. Otherwise Rob allowed nature to take its course.*]

[*Tim had now compiled a 7-1 won-lost record and an impressive 3.04 ERA, thanks in no small part to Rob's score keeping with the amazing multi-colored pen.*]

TIM: Geez, Rob, I have no idea why Rafner is struggling. It's baffling, he seems to be cruising along effortlessly and then he'll suddenly lose command to one hitter, walk him and then groove one right down the middle and "Pow!" A two run homer.

ROB: It is weird, isn't it? And then, as soon as he does, he regains his overpowering stuff and mows everyone down.

[*Rob, on occasion, could not resist tinkering with Rafner's effectiveness, but, of course, was not about to admit that to Tim and Jenny.*]

[*However, Rob, so in love with Lauren and with everything going smoothly in their relationship, ceases pre-scoring any of Nick Rafner's innings, no longer feeling malice. Despite that, Rafner, now having lost confidence during his baffling struggles, seems to have difficulty in regaining the command and control of his pitches.*]

[*Unfortunately for Phoebe, Nick already with a dark side to his character, becomes even more morose and sullen. Rafner could never accept what he conceived as failure or criticism and began lashing at the media and unfortunately, Phoebe.*]

JENNY: So, when do we have the privilege of encountering the goddess of the universe?

ROB: [*laughing*] Lauren is eagerly awaiting meeting you two. I've regaled her with many tales of the adventures of Tim and Jenny.

JENNY: I am hopeful you haven't cast any aspersions as to our character.

ROB: [*laughing*] Heavens, no!

TIM: [*cautiously*] Um, Rob. Jenny and I have heard some rumors regarding Rafner and Phoebe. They're not good, especially for Phoebe.

JENNY: Yes, apparently he's been abusing her, at least verbally. A few of the girls even said he's come home drunk and criticized the way she'd acted, the way she dressed and berated her, especially after a rough outing at the ballpark.

ROB: [*solemn*] That's really too bad. She doesn't deserve that.

TIM: Well, when she dumped you, Rob, we told her she was making a huge error. For an intelligent young woman, she was fairly obstinate and downright stupid, truthfully.

JENNY: When we foretold this very occurrence, Phoebe was fully aware, of course, that we were close friends and therefore, suspected complicity.

ROB: At the time of our breakup, the words that were most hurtful was when Phoebe exclaimed that Rafner was not, get this, "boring." She actually stated that she loved the fact that Nick was unpredictable and exciting.

TIM: Yeah, how did that work out? She made a huge mistake, Rob, and now she's paying dearly.

[*Jenny changes the subject, sensing that the mood has become morose.*]

JENNY: Never mind that, I'm so thrilled that Lauren has found you!

ROB: And I'm so thrilled that I've found Lauren.

[*Rob no longer harbors any resentment towards Phoebe. In fact, just last week at the ballpark, their paths crossed and they exchanged cordial hellos.*]

Fade to black.

Fade in

Int: Rob's apartment in Providence–early June

Rob has just hung up the phone with Lauren, a nightly occurrence on those evenings they don't see each other. Rob's apartment has been re-modeled into a wheelchair accessible apartment.

Rob and Lauren have still not gone beyond petting, as Rob senses her re-luctance and accurately suspected that Lauren was still a virgin. Despite wanting desperately to make love to her, Rob bides his time, knowing fully well that this is the love of his life. Just holding Lauren in his arms would suffice at the time. Rob even obtained a second wheelchair for Lauren's visits.

Rob's doorbell rings and Rob opens the door and sees Phoebe.

ROB: [*taken aback*] Phoebe?

[*Rob stands transfixed inside his apartment for several moments until Phoebe is forced to break the silence.*]

PHOEBE: [*plaintively*] Um, Rob, may I come in?

ROB: Of course, I'm so sorry, I'm just surprised to see you.

[*Surprise, in truth, is an understatement. Shock is more appropriate.*]

[*Phoebe takes a seat on a sectional sofa while Rob takes a seat in a re-cliner across the room.*]

[The two exchange inane and entirely innocuous pleasantries until....]

PHOEBE: *[suddenly blurting out]* Rob, you were so right, I should have listened to you. Nick is a total jerk. I don't know if I can put up with him much longer.

ROB: *[sincerely]* I'm really sorry to hear that. I really hope that things improve for you.

[Phoebe is disappointed to hear Rob's response. She would have preferred to be admonished and perhaps even berated for being so ignorant. She is, in fact, hopeful, that Rob would implore her to come back, since she is not at all aware of his relationship with Lauren.]

PHOEBE: It's been a nightmare, Rob. He's constantly coming in at all hours of the night, usually drunk. He scolds me for no reason and his binge drinking is getting out of control. His temper is awful. He throws things, breaking them.

ROB: I wish there was something I could do or say, Phoebe, but you cannot teach maturity. Hell, I hope that he comes to grips with how he's affecting you.

PHOEBE: It's worse than that, Rob. I've found condoms in his coat pockets and there are frequent calls from strange women late at night. He tells me "it was a wrong number," but only after long, hushed conversations.

[For the next hour, Phoebe pours her heart out to Rob, fervently wishing that he'd offer to take her back, to no avail. Finally, Rob yawns and suggests...]

ROB: *[politely]* Well, it's getting late.

PHOEBE: *[apologetically]* Oh, I'm sorry. I'd best be going.

[*Phoebe is so engrossed in her own travails, that she has not noticed the changes in the apartment. Suddenly she takes the time to peer around the room. She notices the wheelchair ramp in the kitchenette and the folded wheelchair leaning up against the dining room wall.*]

PHOEBE: Wow, major modifications, Rob.

[*Phoebe assumes that the alterations were made to accommodate Rob's uncle, Jim, a war veteran, whom of course, she had met, and whose van Rob had borrowed for his initial date with Lauren.*]

[*Rob is not about to inform Phoebe about Lauren.*]

ROB: Good luck. I'm sure I'll see you at the ballpark.

[*As Rob re-locks the door, he is amazed at how Phoebe has become almost a total stranger to him.*]

Fade out.

Scene Forty-six

Fade in:

[Int: Rob's apartment–Saturday morning early June]

[Rob, now joyful and confident that his lifelong dreams have been fulfilled by the dawning of his chance encounter with Lauren, shifts his attention towards finding out why he had been chosen as the beneficiary of the unusual and powerful gift he had received from the dark stranger at the bar.]

[Rob frequently awakes in the dead of night and wonders just why he was bequeathed such a potent and literally game changing instrument. Rob was never an aggressive individual and therefore wonders if he had unknowingly arrived at some deal with the devil, himself! Was this some sort of a demented "Damn Yankees" Joe Hardy type arrangement?]

[Rob, both bemused and even frightened by the unusual powers he has somehow unwittingly inherited, awakes one morning and becomes entirely resolute to investigate the wherefores and whys.]

[However, Rob wants to remain anonymous for obvious reasons. First, he does not desire to be fitted for a strait jacket and does not wish to be discovered. No one, other than himself, is aware of the pen, not Lauren, not Tim nor Jenny.]

[Rob sits at his computer and searches online in regard to the history of writing instruments, to no avail. It appears as what he now has in his possession is entirely unique.]

[Then he notices an article in the New York Times, about an upcoming "Artifacts and Antique Show" in Portland, Maine. The article reported that authorities of all memorabilia categories would be on hand to buy, sell, appraise and authenticate every conceivable type of memorabilia

123

known to mankind. The event was reported the Times to be the largest show of its kind in any venue.]

[Rob leaves his apartment early on Saturday morning for the trip to Maine.]

[He figures it is worth a shot and the fact that the show is a considerable distance from Providence makes him feel more secure that he will not draw attention to the potent pen.]

[Obviously, he is NOT about to inform any "expert" exactly what his prized possession had accomplished.]

Fade out.

Fade in

[*Superimpose: artifacts and antiques exposition–Portland, ME.*]

[*Arriving at the large auditorium in Portland, Rob pays the admission and with the pen safely tucked in his jacket pocket, begins to explore the voluminous gathering of patrons and dealers. Rob had arrived at 10:00 AM as the doors had opened.*]

[*As Rob walks around the cavernous room, he is astounded by the wide range of collectibles from a vast array of locales. Rob comes across items from seemingly every conceivable historical event in history. He observes Civil War relics as well as memorabilia from both World Wars. He sees ancient books and magazines and vast collections of rare jewelry including rings, watches and pendants. There are art books and various paintings.*]

[*Somewhat in awe, Rob examines the many displays he comes across. Rob shows several dealers his pen and several are intrigued, however, have no clue as to its derivation.*]

[*Several dealers are impressed and intrigued by its inherent splendor, but none could identify its origin. Several comment in regard to its magnificent design, but cannot shed light on its background.*]

[*Rob glances at his watch. It is now approaching 1:00 PM and Rob has been at the show for nearly three hours. Since he has a dinner date with Lauren, Rob sighs.*]

ROB: [*thinking to himself*] Oh well, I didn't learn anything about the pen, but at least I enjoyed seeing all of the splendid artifacts.

[*Rob had just concluded a conversation with a renowned jewelry expert named George, who attempted in vain to shed any light in regard to Rob's pen, so Rob reasoned that he had exhausted all possibilities and prepares to leave the auditorium.*]

[*Rob did notice, however, that a sports memorabilia dealer at the table to the left of the jewelry guru had watched his conversation with great interest. Rob had not even considered presenting the pen for his perusal since he reasoned that such a dealer would not be a logical choice to appraise an apparently ancient pen.*]

[*Rob had noticed the sports memorabilia dealer's vast and impressive collection of photographs, especially the astounding array of old time baseball of the early and mid- Twentieth Century. There were photos of the great Philadelphia Athletics teams, photos of the great New York Yankees teams of the 1920s and '30s, featuring "Babe" Ruth and Lou Gehrig, as well as photos of the legendary St. Louis Cardinals "Gas House Gang." Rob particularly loved the sepia photographs.*]

[*Normally, Rob would have spent an inordinate amount of time inspecting these great historical pieces of baseball's storied past, however, he was preoccupied with learning about his powerful pen.*]

[*The sports memorabilia dealer's voice surprises Rob. RICHARD BRANDON (51) suddenly interrupts.*]

RICHARD BRANDON: Excuse me, sir. I could not help but overhearing your conversation with George in regard to your pen. My name is Richard Brandon. I'd be extremely interested in seeing it up close.

[*Rob turns and faces the friendly sounding dealer. Rob extends his hand.*]

ROB: Hi, I'm Rob Morgan.

[*With that, Rob reaches into his pocket and hands the pen to Richard. Richard closely examines the pen, revolves it several times and appears somewhat astonished.*]

RICHARD BRANDON: [*excitedly*] Fascinating, absolutely fascinating! This particular item is one of the more unusual and captivating items I've seen in years!

[*Rob is taken aback, after all, there were rare photos of Babe Ruth, Lou Gehrig, Jimmy Foxx, Ty Cobb, Walter Johnson and many other greats of the game hanging behind him. What could he possibly know about a pen?!*]

ROB: [*quizzically*] Do you know anything of its origin?

RICHARD BRANDON: [*pausing, deep in thought*] This is one of the most amazing reproductions I've ever seen and I consider myself an authority on the subject. Hold on for a second, I have something to show you.

[*Richard turns and begins to search through a stack of mounted photographs which are piled in a huge box behind him.
Finally, he locates the desired item.*]

RICHARD BRANDON: Here, Rob. Take a look at this.

[*Richard Brandon places a 11" X 16" mounted photograph on the table in front of Rob. It is a color photograph of Babe Ruth seated at a table and "The Bambino" is apparently signing a document, his 1932 contract. Also in the photograph, standing behind "The Babe's" left shoulder, is Ed Barrow, the estimable General Manager of the New York Yankees.*]

[*It is, however, what appeared in Babe Ruth's left hand which immediately receives Rob's immediate and rapt attention. The pen! Rather conspicuously clutched in Babe Ruth's left hand appeared to be the pen which was now in Rob's possession!*]

ROB: [*incredulously*] Are you serious, Richard? Is this actually the same pen?

RICHARD BRANDON: [*laughing*] Actually, no, Rob. As I stated earlier, this is one of the most incredibly realistic appearing reproductions I've ever encountered.

ROB: [*confused*] How can you be certain it isn't the original?

RICHARD BRANDON: Well, I'll say this. This is an incredible likeness, a wonderful replica. It almost even fooled me! Whoever constructed this marble masterpiece and recreated its entire design and glow, went through a great deal of trouble, however, neglected its most vital aspect.

[*Richard then holds the pen up to the light before continuing.*]

RICHARD BRANDON: The purpose of a pen, of course, is to write. Take a close look at the photograph, Rob. You'll notice that Ruth is actually signing the contract in ink and that the point is visible. If you look closely at the pen in your possession, there is nothing to depress or retract the pen. In fact, there is not even a place for a cartridge. This pen is merely a decorative "knock- off." It is extraordinary though and a great conversation piece.

[*Richard Brandon hesitates before continuing.*]

RICHARD BRANDON: Rob, did you also notice that the photograph is a rare color photo? It wasn't until 1928 that Kodak introduced Kodacolor 16mm.

[*Rob, of course, is not about to allow the dealer to learn that his pen indeed, is capable of writing and that it appeared to only write when he, himself, pointed it at his scorecards!*]

[*Rob is now convinced that he possessed an extremely precious, strange but powerful instrument. But why?! Why was he chosen and by whom was he chosen?*]

ROB: Thanks for you invaluable information, Richard.

[*Rob takes one of Richard Brandon's cards since he is interested in perhaps purchasing some archival baseball photos in the future. Rob turns and begins to walk towards the exit of the auditorium in order to drive back in time for his date with Lauren, when Richard interrupts.*]

RICHARD BRANDON: [*calling out*] Rob, I'd be interested in purchasing your item anyhow. Although it isn't authentic, it would make a great addition to the photo of Babe Ruth signing his contract. I'll give you $200 for it.

ROB: [*smiling*] Thanks, but I think I'll hold onto it for a while. It was a gift.

RICHARD BRANDON: I understand. If you change your mind, just give me a call. Good luck and nice meeting you.

ROB: Likewise.

Fade out.

Fade in

Int: Susan And Lauren's home–late Saturday afternoon

Rob arrives in Narragansett to pick Lauren up in order to take her to the Bays game at Ben Mondor Stadium. This is the initial time that Lauren will meet Tim and Jenny. Lauren is thrilled about the prospect of meeting them.

Lauren wears a blue and red frilly dress and a Bays baseball cap sits atop her beautiful brunette hair. The evening is warm and dry and even more exciting is that Tim Barrett is the starting pitcher.

ROB: God, you look exquisite!

LAUREN: [*laughing*] You always say that. [*pausing*] But you had better always say it!

[*As Lauren is assisted to her seat directly behind home plate, many of the players wives and girlfriends take notice. As Rob gently helps Lauren into her seat, the parade began. The first to arrive is MILAGROS RODRI-GUEZ (27), Eddy's petite and attractive wife.*]

MILAGROS: [*excitedly*] So, this is Lauren! Señor Robbie, Lauren es muy hermosa. You weren't kidding, you sly dog!

LAUREN: Thank you so much, Milagros.

MILAGROS: You can call be "Milly," sweetheart.

[*Milagros then turns to Rob.*]

MILAGROS: You must bring her to dinner, Rob. Mi casa es su casa, mi querida.

[*Patricia Wiggins, Lionel's wife then approaches.*]

PATRICIA: Hi, Lauren. Gosh, you really are a knockout! I thought that Rob was exaggerating about your beauty, honey. No one could possibly be that gorgeous. If anything, he underestimated your looks, you're absolutely precious! Welcome to the family.

LAUREN: [*blushing*] Thank you so much, Pat.

[*Jenny approached from the other side of the aisle and places her hand on Lauren's shoulder.*]

JENNY: Hello, Lauren, I'm Jenny Barrett.

[*Lauren turns and both see each other for the initial time.*]

LAUREN: [*thrilled*] Oh, Jenny, this is an honor! I've heard so much about you and Tim!

[*Jenny, lovely herself, is practically dumbstruck by Lauren's immense and improbable beauty.*]

JENNY: Oh, my God! I've encountered a Miss Universe!

LAUREN: [*embarrassed and laughing*] Not quite, I can assure you.

[*Jenny, never at a loss for words, counters.*]

JENNY: We'll gather at the end of this evening's proceedings for some libations and we'll discuss in length this cradle robbing pervert and also de-

131

bate various means in which you can avoid the reprobate in the future as allowed by statute.

[*Lauren laughs uproariously as she hears firsthand that all the tales she'd heard regarding the former Jennifer Volkov, were all true.*]

[*The usher arrives and begins to fold up Lauren's wheelchair in preparation of returning it to the players family room as Phoebe makes her entrance. Phoebe, dressed professionally in a pants suit, looking very much like the lady Rob had known in now what seemed like ages ago, notices the clutter of people around Rob. Phoebe then sees the usher removing the wheelchair.*]

[*With all of the activity surrounding Lauren, Rob is completely oblivious of Phoebe's arrival. Finally, as everyone settles down in their respective seats, Phoebe sees at once what the commotion is all about.*]

[*The realization hits Phoebe like a ton of bricks, the wheelchair ramp in the kitchenette, the wheelchair propped up against the dining room wall, obviously not belonging to Rob's uncle, Jim.*]

[*Then Phoebe sees Lauren's face for the initial time. Phoebe sits stunned by Lauren's unworldly beauty. Phoebe then sees Rob's face and sees at once that he is hopelessly in love.*]

[*On the evening she had visited Rob's apartment and spilled her heart out to him, she had entertained thoughts of getting back together with him, but now sadly realizes why Rob had made no effort to encourage her.*]

[*As disappointed as Phoebe is to realize exactly what she had thrown away, she also had heartfelt gladness for Rob.*]

[*Just before the game, in a move that catches everyone off guard, Phoebe arises from her seat and walks over to Rob and Lauren.*]

PHOEBE: [*sincerely*] Hello, I'm Phoebe Rains. I wish you a lifetime of great health and happiness.

LAUREN: [*smiling and gracious*] Thank you, Phoebe, I'm Lauren Bartlett. That's really sweet of you. It's really nice to meet you.

[*Lauren is somewhat aware of Rob's former relationship with Phoebe.*]

[*When Phoebe returns to her seat, Patricia Wiggins leans over to speak to Jenny.*]

PATRICIA: [*whispering*] That took a lot of courage. I believe there's hope for that girl.

[*Phoebe leaves in the third inning of the game. However, she makes it a point to smile and wave to Lauren as she leaves.*]

[*Little does anyone know, but that would be the very last time anyone would see Phoebe Rains at the ballpark.*]

[*Meanwhile, Lauren's "debut" with the Providence Bays is going perfectly. Lauren, absolutely radiant, her baseball cap playfully turned slightly askew by Patricia Wiggins, "You go girl!) Does not straighten out her cap, but rather wears it sideways as a badge of honor.*]

[*Lauren basks in the warm glow from the affection showered upon her by the family of the ball club. That, and the comfortable, cloudless starlit evening provides her with a security blanket that makes her tingle. With Rob at her side, she is in the midst of experiencing the pure happiness she only knew as a child.*]

[*The game itself is going well for the Bays and for Tim Barrett. Tim, without any assistance from Rob's pen which still rests in his pocket, retires 18 of the first 21 hitters he faces and enjoys a 4-1 lead.*]

[*Rob, in recent weeks, had seldom used the pen, but despite that, Tim Barrett had indeed, resurrected his career.*]

[*However, in the top of the seventh inning, Tim is digging himself a hole.*]

[*With one out, Tim allows two hard hit line drive singles to the second and third place hitters in the Washington Nationals batting order and now faced the prospect of having to pitch to their fearsome clutch hitting outfielder, the powerful DeJuan Washington, the leading home run hitter in the league.*]

[*As Washington stands menacingly at the plate, representing the game tying run, Rob ponders the predicament.*]

[*Rob, of course, had still not informed Lauren of his meeting with the dark, mysterious stranger or the magical pen, however, had planned to do so within the following few weeks since their relationship had reached a point where Lauren knew that Rob was a down to earth person, not given to sensationalist drivel.*]

[*Of course, now was NOT the time, however, to inform Lauren that he was about to extricate his buddy, Tim, out of a tight situation on the ball field with a "magic pen."*]

[*So, with Tim in desperate need of a nicely turned 5-4-3 double play, Rob reaches into his pocket for the glistening, game altering pen. Rob is considering what a downer it would be if the Bays lost on Lauren's debut with the team.*]

[*Lauren, not a novice, is somewhat aware of how to score a baseball game, therefore, Rob, not wanting to shock her by seeing a premature entry onto his scorecard, angles the scorecard away from her.*]

[*Rob is poised to make the entry when Lauren, suddenly feels a chill despite the warm evening. Lauren looks down to adjust an afghan which she*

134

had placed over her legs and at once, sees the glistening pen in Rob's right hand.]

LAUREN: [*emitting an audible gasp*]

ROB: [*with great concern*] Lauren, sweetheart, are you all right?

[*Lauren's lips quiver and her entire body shakes.*]

LAUREN: [*softly*] Wh... Where did you get that pen, Rob?

[*Thousands of thoughts flash through Rob's mind in some sort of a surrealistic collage, the mysterious dark man in the bar who the bartender never saw, the very same man insisting Rob not cancel a trip to "the southwest," seeing "Oklahoma" and meeting Lauren, the strange man presenting the glistening pen to Rob and saying, There's a real treasure at the end of the rainbow," the man being aware of Rob's birthday and suggesting "use it judiciously," as he presented Rob with the pen. And now, Lauren, precious Lauren, trembling at the sight of the pen!*]

ROB: [*thinking to himself and nearly panic stricken*] My God, what is going on?!

[*Rob, practically frightened out of his wits, attempts to compose himself.*]

ROB: Lauren, angel, what have I done?

[*For the following several minutes, Rob tells her everything, meeting the man at the bar, the unusual "gift," how the man persuaded Rob to attend the show where he first laid eyes on Lauren and finally the man's parting words, "Use it judiciously."*]

[*Upon hearing the words "Use it judiciously," Lauren still trembles and is visibly shaken as tears well in her extraordinary brown eyes. Lauren then stares down at the pen which Rob had placed in her still trembling*

hands and her thoughts return to her childhood and her father's words,
"Someday, a handsome young prince will call on you, Lauren.
You will know him for he will also possess magic."]

[*Rob is now devastated, never having seen Lauren cry. He watches the tears roll down her cheeks onto her quivering lips, his heart about to break at the sight of her tears.*]

ROB: [*overwhelmed*] Oh, Lauren, angel, what have I done wrong?

[*Lauren squeezes Rob's hand in hers, her strength belying her diminutive size, responds.*]

LAUREN: [*tenderly*] Oh, Rob, my love, Rob my sweet, you've done absolutely nothing wrong. You've done everything right!

[*Rob, completely relieved at seeing the singular shy smile return to Lauren's beautiful face, sighs as he leans over and kisses her cheeks and dries her face by swallowing her tears.*]

ROB: [*whispering*] I love you so much, Lauren.

LAUREN: [*whispering*] I love you, too, Rob. I adore you.

[*Rob is so preoccupied with Lauren, Rob is not even remotely aware that the top of the seventh inning had ended. Before Rob could jot down the 5-4-3 double play which would have extricated Tim Barrett from his precarious situation, he had placed the gleaming pen in Lauren's hand.*]

[*Without the assistance of the "magical pen," the fearsome slugger, DeJuan Washington, had inconceivably grounded into that very 5-4-3 double play!*]

[*Lauren now turned the pen slowly in her hand, seemingly looking for something on it. As she revolves it slowly in her fingers, Rob sees for ini-*]

tial time on the pen, brightly illuminated in the stadium lights, the hidden initials, "L.A.B."]

[Lauren smiles and places the pen in her purse and holds Rob's hand tightly. Rob hoped never to see the pen again. He didn't want the pen, but, oh my, did he want Lauren.]

Fade to black.

Fade in

Superimpose: The home of Nick Rafner and Phoebe Rains

Int: Living room

Phoebe enters the living room as NICK RAFNER (28) sits on a sofa drinking a beer.

PHOEBE: I ran into Rob Morgan at the ballpark today. He's got a beautiful girlfriend. She's wheelchair bound, she seemed very nice.

NICK RAFNER: [*laughing*] He's porking "Old Ironsides," huh? Can't find a full-bodied healthy woman!
[*sardonically*] This Rob guy is a real loser, babe! I can't believe you hooked up with him. What were you thinking?

[*The following morning, without saying a word to Nick, who had left for the ballpark, Phoebe packs her belongings and drives to New York City and begins her life anew.*]

[*As Nick returns home and realizes Phoebe had left, he grabs another beer out of the refrigerator and calls his cohort, Earl Coakely, his only friend on the team.*]

NICK RAFNER: [*bitter*] Fuckin' whore bitch! Good riddance, broads like that are a dime a dozen!

EARL: [*over the phone*] Yeah, Nick, a dime a dozen.

Fade out.

Fade in

Int: Family room at the ball park.

The game ends with a 5-2 victory for the Bays. Tim Barrett is the winning pitcher and big JOHN RAINWATER, the closer, (28) earns the save.

John Rainwater, a thoughtful and huge full blooded Native American, born and raised on an Indian reservation in Washington State, is a soft-spoken and powerful man. At 6'5" tall and 250 lbs, Rainwater is not a man to be trifled with.

Rainwater is a Skagit Indian as was his late father, Jay, a former elder tribesman. John's mother, Mabel, is a Yavapai Indian from Northern Arizona.

John Rainwater seems introverted to those that do not know him well. However, John is proud of his heritage. John became aware at a very early age that life on the reservation could prove hard as poverty, despair and alcoholism was not a stranger to many of his peers.

Before white people settled in Washington State, the Skagit Indians prided themselves in being self-sufficient, food was abundant and the Native Americans were incredible fishermen. Soon, the white settlers invaded the territory and in the process, took over the entire fishing industry, taking away the livelihood of the Native Americans. The newcomers also claimed their ancestral homes and forced the Skagit Indians to relocate. Stripped of their dignity, their customs and their heritage and forced to ignore and abandon their very own cultural and educational ways, the life of the Native Americans was often difficult.

John Rainwater loved the act of hurling a baseball in anger. It relaxed him. As much as living on the reservation as a youngster depressed him, as a now 28 year-old man, he could hardly wait for the baseball season to conclude, so that he could once more return to his home and his people.

Rainwater, a quiet and unassuming individual, mostly kept to himself on the ball club, some thinking him aloof. However, he really enjoyed the company of Tim, Jenny and Rob and often invited them to fish with them on the reservation during the off-season. What he most admired about Tim, Jenny and Rob was that they asked no personal questions and when fishing only kept what they would eat, the overabundance being returned to the Skagit River.

The first player to arrive in the family room after showering is John Rainwater, who had struck out the side in the ninth to preserve Tim Barrett's victory. Rainwater made it a point to go over to where Lauren is seated in her wheelchair, still clutching Rob's hand.

The huge Native American studies Lauren's face before speaking.

JOHN RAINWATER: [*softly*] Rob, so this is Lauren. I could not help but notice you behind the screen. Young lady, there is a glow surrounding you. You have been blessed by the spirits.

LAUREN: [*blushing*] Thank you, so much, John. I've heard many great things about you from Rob, and I too, sense your spirituality.

[*John Rainwater kneels down in front of Lauren, studies her face even longer and then continues.*]

JOHN RAINWATER: There is Native American blood rolling through your veins, perhaps from a prior life.

[*With that, John Eagle Rainwater reaches around his own neck and removes a colorful turquoise beaded necklace and places it around Lauren's neck.*]

JOHN RAINWATER: The spiritual symbols and the mere fashioning of these beads required a sacred task. These will assist in both healing and curing. Please wear these, Lauren. The spirits will protect you. You are about to experience a rite of passage.
Share these when necessary, you will know when the time is right.

LAUREN: [*in total sincerity*] Thank you so much, John.

JOHN RAINWATER: [*smiling broadly*] The pleasure is entirely mine. [*pauses*] Oh, if you and Rob can find the time to join us on the reservation this fall, we'd be honored to have you.

ROB AND LAUREN: [*simultaneously*] We'd love to!

[*Both Rob and Lauren giggle at the exact timing of their response. John Rainwater turns and says over his shoulder.*]

JOHN RAINWATER: Great minds think alike. The timing of your replies was no coincidence.

[*DANNY GONSALVES (31) the catcher, was the next to greet Lauren.*]

[*Danny's brother, Cesar, had been shot and severely wounded during a drive-by shooting in East Los Angeles as a seven year-old. Cesar, of course, was an innocent bystander in an act of senseless violence.*]

[*Cesar, a paraplegic, went on to become an inspiration in his community, graduated from U.C.L.A. with honors and delivered lectures regarding street gangs and violence.*]

[*Danny Gonsalves had heard about Lauren, however, being the catcher, had his back to the screen all night, therefore, he had yet to see her.*]

[*As he enters the room, seeing the beautiful girl in her wheelchair, his heart immediately goes out to her, thinking about his brother, Cesar.*]

[*Danny, of course, had encountered many wheelchair bound people and had never hesitated in approaching them. With no lack of understanding their situations, Danny was most comfortable with them since he spent an inordinate amount of time discussing their anxieties, depression, apprehension, fears and misconceptions that most folks had about them.*]
[*Danny did hours of community work with his brother, Cesar.*]

[*Danny Gonsalves kneels at Lauren's feet and takes her hands in his.*]

DANNY GONSALVES: Mi amor, Lauren, it is an honor and pleasure to meet you, you are so beautiful. When you are done with this ugly cabron, Rob, please call me. We will make lots of good looking wheelchair babies together. With this feo *(ugly)* Rob guy, you can only make ugly babies like him.

[*Lauren tossed her head back and laughs loudly. With his total lack of inhibition, Danny had disarmed her.*]

[*Danny then turns to Rob.*]

DANNY GONSALVES: [*attempting to look serious*] Rob, you are one lucky man. You are extremely fortunate that this beautiful young woman is blind.

[*Later that evening, Rob, Lauren, Tim, Jenny, Eddy and Milly, all gather at Gregg's Restaurant in Warwick, where all shared laughter, camaraderie and all involved absolutely adored Lauren.*]

[*Later that evening, Rob and Lauren make love for the initial time. Within weeks, Rob and Lauren were engaged to be married.*]

Fade out.

Fade in:

Superimpose: Providence news station-late September

A sportscaster delivers the 6:00 News.

SPORTSCASTER: Well, the news on Providence Bays right-hander, Nick Rafner, is not good. An already disappointing season for Rafner turned even more dismal with the announcement that Rafner has been charged with assaulting a man at a San Diego nightclub. According to police reports, Rafner allegedly groped a woman at the lounge and when her husband came to her defense, Rafner attacked him, knocking him unconscious and breaking his jaw.

Rafner, who witnesses claimed was inebriated, was arrested and released on his own recognizance. Earlier this season it was reported that a 22 year-old woman in Chicago had announced that Rafner had fathered her child, a claim the huge pitcher categorically denied, but has since agreed to pay child support. And now this.

What began as a promising season for Nick Rafner has apparently deteriorated into a sordid mess. There are now rumors that Rafner, who is a free agent at the end of this campaign, will not be offered a contract.

[*Nick Rafner was now convinced that Rob had somehow influenced Phoebe into leaving him and vowed to exact revenge.*]

[*Rob and Lauren meanwhile, were planning their wedding and subsequent honeymoon. A wedding at "The Coast Guard House" in Narragansett, where Lauren's mom and dad had met, was scheduled and the couple planned to depart immediately depart on a cross-country trip in their van.*]

[*Plans were finalized to make stops at national parks, national monuments and places Lauren had always dreamed of visiting.*]

[*The wedding was to take place the Saturday after the baseball season concluded. Therefore, they'd depart the following morning on their journey.*]

[*The baseball season rolled into its final stages, the leaves displayed a tinge of early color and fall was in the breeze. The Bays, although a good ball club, were not quite good enough to reach the post-season.*]

[*Still, Tim Barrett compiled a solid 17-8 record with a stellar 3.16 Earned run average, despite the fact that Rob had not used, or even seen the glistening pen since that fateful day in June.*]

Fade out.

Fade in

Int: Lauren and Susan's home in Narragansett–late September

On the morning of the last game of the baseball season, a home game for the Bays and six days before the wedding, Rob sits in Susan's kitchen having breakfast with Lauren. Lauren is to stay home that day, preparing for the wedding, catering to out of town guests while her mom assisted her in packing for her cross-country honeymoon.

As Rob readies himself to leave for the afternoon finale on the bright, but chilly day, Lauren feels a distinct chill and shivers suddenly. As Rob kisses her on the cheek and begins walking towards the door, Lauren suddenly and anxiously calls out to him.

LAUREN: [*with deep concern*] Rob, please wait! Here!

[*Reaching around her neck, Lauren removes the beaded turquoise necklace given to her months before by John Eagle Rainwater. She places it around Rob's neck and kisses him.*]

LAUREN: [*softly, but seriously*] Here, leave this on today. Promise me that you will.

ROB: [*laughing*] Of course I will, my love. Lauren, don't look so serious.

[*Lauren appears to be agitated and uneasy.*]

LAUREN: [*sternly*] Promise me that you will!

[*Rob is confused by Lauren's sudden abnormal behavior, so he changes to a more serious demeanor.*]

ROB: [*assuredly*] Alright, Angel, I promise.

LAUREN: [*purring softly*] That's much better, my love. That's much better.

Fade out.

Fade in

Int: The Providence Bays clubhouse

Nick Rafner sits in front of his locker, a can of beer in his hand, mumbling and cursing. Rafner had just been informed by management that the ball club would not be picking up his option for the following season and had no intention of re- signing him. His career with the Providence Bays, and perhaps his major league career, was for all intents and purposes, over.

Word spread quickly throughout the clubhouse after Rafner's lone friend on the team, Earl Coakely complained that his buddy was being screwed.

Rafner was told that he'd become a distraction on and off the field. Bottom line, an 11-16 won-lost record with a rather unimpressive 5.02 ERA.

[Rob is allowed into the locker room by Clubhouse Custodian, ELMER EIFERT (63). He is on his way to Tim's locker to congratulate him on a great season when the abrasive voice of Nick Rafner stopped him in his tracks.

Of course, Rob has no idea that Rafner had been handed his walking papers.

NICK RAFNER: [*derisively*] Hey, Rob, still banging the cripple? Can't find a two-legged woman to get it on with?

[*Rob glares at the huge right-hander who sits with clenched fists and outweighs Rob by some sixty pounds.*]

NICK RAFNER: [*malevolently*] Why don't you bring her in here and I'll hang her off a rack and I'll have a go at her, too!

[*As Nick Rafner grins and sneers at him, Rob, enraged, charges at Rafner, who had hoped for that very reaction from the much smaller man.*]

[*Two quick, solid punches land on Rob's cheek and jaw and send him sprawling to the ground.*]

[*Realizing immediately that their friend, Rob, was in over his head, Tim, Les Cameron, Lionel Wiggins, Eddy Rodriguez and Danny Gonsalves all attempt to come to his aide, however, a mysterious force seems to freeze them where they stand.*]

[*Meanwhile, John Eagle Rainwater, sits in front of his locker, stripped to the waist, in a lotus position on his stool.*]

[*Rainwater sits, his muscles bulging, his arms at his sides, staring straight up at the ceiling, as if in a trance. Beads of sweat form on Rainwater's brow as he grinds his teeth.*]

[*Rob, hurting badly, picks himself off the floor and throws a desperate wild right hand which Rafner easily avoids and then sends Rob to the floor once more with a combination of powerful punches.*]

[*Now, as Rafner stands over Rob, he reaches back into his locker and pulls out a knife.*]

NICK RAFNER: You're a dead man, you little prick!

[*Suddenly, Rafner stops in his tracks. Rafner stares down at Rob, who is semi-conscious.*]

NICK RAFNER: What the fuck is that?!

[*Rafner then howls in derision.*] Aw, look. The little faggot wears a pretty necklace, how cute!

[*Rafner, the knife in his right hand, reaches down with his left to yank the beaded necklace off of Rob's neck.*]

NICK RAFNER: I'll fucking kill you, you little queer!

[*Across the room, John Eagle Rainwater still sits in a fist- clenched trance, the sweat now literally poring off of him, forming a puddle beneath his stool.*]

[*As Nick Rafner grabbed the necklace, a loud audible crackling noise fills the room. The necklace sizzles in Rafner's hand, which he recoils immediately, Rafner's flesh burning.*]

NICK RAFNER: [*in anguish*] Owwwwww!!! What the fuck?!

[*As Rafner attempts to raise his right hand which still held the knife, he realizes it is frozen in place, seemingly like stone.*]

[*Rob clears his head and is now on his feet and lands a perfect left hook squarely on Rafner's jaw, knocking the huge pitcher backwards. Rob follows with a straight right hand to Rafner's nose and another devastating left hook that lands on Rafner's ear. Rafner staggers.*]

[*Rob stares down at his fists. They seem foreign to him, like anvils. Rob is conjuring up thoughts about Popeye and spinach. Rafner injured, now spits at Rob. Rob, reacts to the projectile as if it's in slow motion and easily avoids it and it lands squarely on Earl Coakely's face.*]

[*Coakely is standing just a few feet away, but seemed to be firmly in place like a marble statue.*]

[*Rob then lands the finishing blow, a thunderous uppercut, which lands on Rafner's chin, literally lifting the hulking man off the ground and into a large laundry bin containing dirty warm-up clothing.*]

[*Across the locker room, John Rainwater, his fever now broken, emerges from his trance. The entire team now advances towards the carnage.*]

[*Tim Barrett peers down at the semi-conscious Rafner, bends at the waist, doffs his cap and begins.*]

Fade out.

Fade in

TIM: [*smiling broadly*] I bid you a not so fond adieu, you worthless elongated turd.

[*Tim thinks about how Jenny would have loved his soliloquy.*]

[*Nick Rafner, now semi-alert, his mouth slightly agape, has a blank look on his face.*]

[*Danny Gonsalves, sizes up the situation and puts his arm around Rob's shoulder.*]

DANNY GONSALVES: [*smiling broadly*] Jesus, Rob, you're a beast. Remind me not to piss you off.

[*Nick Rafner slowly and awkwardly climbs out of the bin, dusts himself off and ambles out of the locker room and into the street in full uniform.*]

NICK RAFNER: [*mumbling*] Worst fucking dream I ever had.

Fade out.

Fade in:

Int: Susan and Lauren's home later that evening

After the game, Rob arrives at the Bartlett home in Narragansett. Rob gently removes the beaded turquoise necklace and replaces it around Lauren's neck.

Rob studies Lauren's face, but doesn't say anything. Not a word is spoken as Lauren's eyes seem to gleam and sparkle more than ever and her facial expression is that of a Cheshire cat.

Fade out.

Fade in

Superimpose: Earlier that day before the game

Ext: Outside the gates of Ben Mondor Stadium

A rookie reporter (BRIAN WILKINS (24) busies himself by interviewing Bays fans that are arriving to see the last game of the season. The novice correspondent is not familiar with any of the fans or the players' wives, so he has no idea what is in store as he comes upon the former Jenny Volkov, the erudite and often verbose wife of Tim Barrett.

Brian Wilkins, microphone in hand, approaches the attractive Jenny and asks.

BRIAN WILKINS: So, how would you assess the 2028 season and what hopes do you have for the 2029 campaign?

JENNY: [*ebullient*] It's difficult to convey a substantive reply since it would no doubt encourage someone to immediate expostulate, thereby nullifying and invalidating my opinion which is merely suppositional, and while I'm not attempting to engage in subterfuge, there are few definitive answers to your query. Under normal circumstances, I'm not given to hyperbole although I'm generally inclined to panegyric.

[*Brian Wilkins, rookie reporter, stares at little Jenny incredulously. There is a vacuous look on his face which Jenny immediately senses. Jenny, still a ball buster after all these years, then concludes.*]

JENNY: In other words, I really don't fucking know.

[*Jenny then trots off happily as the reporter remains frozen in place, apparently in shock.*]

[*At that moment, Tim Barrett walks by. Of course, the inexperienced reporter is aware of who Tim is, therefore he quickly recovers, thrusts the microphone in Tim's face and asks the very same question he had asked Jenny.*]

[*Unknown to the rookie reporter, Tim, standing twenty feet away, had witnessed his wife respond to the question.*]

[*So, as Brian Wilkins awaits Tim Barrett's reply, Tim just points to Jenny, who is now merrily skipping off to the players family room and replies.*]

TIM: [*pointing towards Jenny*] What she said.

[*The newcomer, Brian Wilkins, is not having a good day.*]

Fade out.

Fade in

Int: The Coast Guard House the following Saturday

The spectacular wedding takes place the following Saturday on a perfect fall like afternoon that shone with brilliant colors.

As Lauren, wearing white, wheels down the aisle, Rob falls in love all over again, still not being able to comprehend her unworldly beauty. Tim Barrett, the best man, produces the ring from his pocket and the marriage is consecrated.

The ensuing honeymoon takes the young couple to International Falls, Coeur d' Alene, Idaho, Whitefish, Montana, "Big Sky Country," Glacier National Park and up into the Canadian Rockies, Yellowstone National Park, Bryce Canyon in Utah, Boynton Canyon in Sedona, Arizona, the Grand Canyon, and of course, a visit to the Skagit Indian Reservation in Washington State.]

Fade to black.

Fade in

Superimpose: Two weeks later

Int: Rob & Lauren's brand new home in Narragansett

On the day they return to their brand new home on the coast of Narragansett, Rhode Island, Lauren awakes late that moonlit night, leaving Rob alone in bed.

Removing the brilliant pen from her purse, she draws a picture of herself dancing on the beach. However, she also adds Rob to the painting.

Lauren wheels herself back to bed and climbs in next to Rob and quickly falls asleep.

That night, for the first time since she was eleven years-old, Lauren dreams of dancing and running on the beach, this time with Rob. Rob, too, experiences the very same incredibly vivid dream as he holds Lauren as they dance beneath thousands of indescribably beautifully bright stars.

In the dream, the tide is out and as they prance and run, a man wearing a trench coat sits on a nearby seawall, his collar turned up, watching them.

Lauren, while out of bed, had also drawn a painting of her mom, Susan, also walking on the beach, except Lauren embellishes the painting by adding another person walking hand in hand with her mom.

Early that morning, Susan Bartlett, exactly as her daughter had done earlier, has a wonderfully vivid dream. And like her daughter, Lauren, in her dream, Susan Bartlett, too, was not alone.

Fade to black.

Fade in:

Superimpose: seven years later, Narragansett-2035

Int: Susan Bartlett's home in Narragansett

Seven years passed since Rob and Lauren had married and Susan Bartlett, Lauren's mom, still an extremely attractive woman, is often encouraged by others, to seek male companionship.

Susan still lives comfortably, however, in her Narragansett home where her three grandchildren often visit with their parents, Rob and Lauren. On occasion, a brilliantly colored pen rests on Susan's desk in her library, placed there by her daughter, Lauren. Susan never lacks for companionship, even when "alone" as the pen is always accompanied by Lauren's gentle instruction.

LAUREN: [*winking at her mom*] Use it judiciously.

Fade to black.

www.ingramcontent.com/pod-product-compliance
Lightning Source LLC
Chambersburg PA
CBHW052007240626
47153CB00008B/2767